By the time Anna Palmitkov's eyes were blinking and she was shaking herself awake, both of her arms and her legs were tied securely to the four-poster bed.

"Bastard, you've broken my neck!" she groaned.

"You're lucky that's all," Carter said.

A string of Russian curses that even Carter didn't know erupted from her mouth.

"You had better kill me, bastard, because if we ever meet again, I'll kill you . . . and as slowly as I can!"

"You know something?" Carter said, stuffing a pair of panties into her mouth, "I believe you . . ."

# NICK CARTER IS IT!

# FROM THE NICK CARTER
# KILLMASTER SERIES

# NICK CARTER

## KILLMASTER

# The Berlin Target

CHARTER BOOKS, NEW YORK

THE BERLIN TARGET

A Charter Book/published by arrangement with
The Condé Nast Publications, Inc.

PRINTING HISTORY
Charter edition/February 1986

ISBN: 0-441-05386-6

Charter Books are published by The Berkley Publishing Group,
200 Madison Avenue, New York, New York 10016.
PRINTED IN THE UNITED STATES OF AMERICA

*Dedicated to the men of the
Secret Services of the
United States of America*

# ONE

It had gone like clockwork so far, but then the beginning of an operation—setting it in motion—was always the easiest part. The biggest hurdles were many and yet to come.

The sky above Sevastopol' was a clear blue, and the sun shining down over "Soviet Florida"—the southern Crimea—was warm. So warm that Nick Carter had removed his well-worn, cracked leather jacket and slung it over his shoulder.

He crossed Nakhimov Square and entered Primorsky Boulevard, the seafront. He passed the museum, the Court's Harbor, home of the Soviet Black Sea fleet, and continued on into the older and dingier section of the city.

Batov Street was little more than an alley leading from the wider boulevard down to the wooden promenade and the sea. It was a street of small cafés, drinking houses, and bistros with cheap sleeping rooms above for one-hour visitors or overnight travelers. Batov Street was a place where workers on vacation or local fishermen could go for cheap vodka, filling food, and inexpensive lodging. If one could afford it, companionship could also be arranged to go with a room.

The name of the place was The Silver Dolphin, and it was easy to spot. Inside, it was a clone of every other place on the street: a wooden bar that was ancient before Peter was czar of

1

all the Russias, a few solid tables and chairs, and cushioned benches along the walls. Even though it was a blistering eighty degrees outside, the ever-present samovar sat steaming away on one corner of the bar.

Carter dropped his bag by the bar and claimed one of the stools. The bartender was an old man with a chest-to-knee apron the color of old concrete. He used a dirty rag to move around the refuse on the bar, and mumbled a greeting.

"Vodka," Carter said.

"*Da.*"

The other male customers in the bar were, for the most part, dressed as was Carter. There were two old peasant women gossiping over tea at one of the tables. The three younger women were working girls, making a little extra money on the weekend.

It was common knowledge—and acceptable in the resort areas—for salesgirls and minor clerks to supplement their incomes with an occasional roll in the hay.

Near the window a fat old man dozed in a chair, a cold glass of tea on the table before him. The cat in his lap stretched out and also slept. Carter guessed that both of them, without opening an eye, could have told him how many buttons he had on his shirt.

The old man could have had "informant" stamped across his forehead.

"Vodka."

"*Spasee'ba*," Carter replied, dropping a bill on the bar. "You have rooms?"

"*Da* . . . for the night?"

"*Da.* I just arrived on the morning train from Khar'kov. I leave in the morning for the workers' camp at Soucha."

"Vacation?"

Carter nodded.

"I will have to have your travel pass and your worker's identification."

Carter passed them over and returned his concentration to the three women. He knew the bartender wouldn't miss it. In minutes the old man was back with the room ticket registration.

Carter scanned it:

> Age: 36
> Place of Birth: Valki
> Place of Residence: 110 Karpolov Prospect, Khar'kov
> Workplace: Fitter, People's Tractor Factory, Khar'kov

Carter scrawled his signature across the bottom of the slip: Mikhail Ivanovich Assalov.

As he did so, he mentioned to the barman what a long, dry, and lonely trip it had been.

The man nodded knowingly. "You wish some company, comrade?"

"You can provide some company?"

He shrugged, his shoulders rising to his ears. "Such a thing, you know, is illegal . . . but I can inform one of the women of your room number."

"The tall brunette with the small breasts," Carter said.

"I will see, comrade."

The woman sat alone at one of the tables, sipping tea and leafing through a magazine. The barman approached her, whispered in her ear, and waited. She looked up at Carter, weighed the price she could ask, and nodded.

"The young lady's name is Ludmilla Alecmovna. For how long would you wish her company, comrade?"

"The night."

"I see. That will be thirty-five rubles, and it includes a bottle."

Carter grimaced but didn't quibble. He paid, grabbed his bag, and followed the man upstairs and into a room.

"The toilet is on the floor above, comrade. Your hours for the bath are between seven and eight this evening and six and seven in the morning." He set the bottle and two glasses on a table.

Carter nodded and thanked him, and the man oozed from the room.

The Killmaster poured three fingers of the white lightning into a glass and moved to the murky window. He sighed as he looked out over the harbor. It had been a long three weeks and seven thousand miles from Washington to where he now stood.

Three weeks previously, to the day, David Hawk had briefed him in the AXE offices high above Dupont Circle in D.C.

"Six months ago, we turned a deep-cover agent named Peter Limpton. His real name is Boris Simonov, and he was operating as an electronics broker for high-level, high-tech equipment manufactured in the United States."

While Hawk had filled him in on the general data, Carter had been scanning the details from the man's dossier.

Peter Limpton's main job was to set up a dummy West German company for the purchase of American electronics equipment. This he had done, plus devised a method and route of diverting this equipment to East Germany and eventually to Moscow.

Just about the time he had everything ready to go, he had been blown and turned. But before Limpton could be used as a double, he had been called back to Moscow. The reason Moscow gave was their sudden decision that Limpton should acquire a wife to help him.

Needless to say, the wife he was to be given was to be a KGB agent even better trained than himself.

But Washington had learned that this wasn't the case at all. In fact, quite the contrary. Limpton would be introduced to his "wife," and they would be given a Black Sea vacation together so they could get to know one another.

"Actually, Nick," Hawk continued, "the new wife will get out of Limpton all the routes and methods, plus the contacts he has made in the States—"

"And then the KGB will execute him," Carter finished.

Hawk nodded. "That's the way we've got it figured. We want all that information ourselves. That's why we've got to get him out."

Limpton and his KGB wife were scheduled for a two-week stay in the southern Crimea at an exclusive VIP resort in the Sochi area.

Two days before, Carter had gone aboard the Turkish liner

*Ilion* in the guise of a stevedore. A special section of the ship's brig had been provided for him during the sail across the Black Sea to Odessa.

But Carter had donned scuba gear and slipped into the sea fifty miles off the coast of the Crimea and Sevastopol'. Within a half hour, he had been picked up by a fishing trawler.

They had everything ready for him: proper clothes, a suitcase with more clothing, identity papers, a travel pass, and a canceled train ticket stub from Khar'kov to Sevastopol'.

The trawler had churned into Sevastopol' harbor just before dawn. Carter had stayed belowdecks until the catch was unloaded, and then had gone ashore at noon as one of the crew.

The boat was a long-range trawler, the *Rosa*, out of Sevastopol', and often cruised the entire length of the Crimean coast in search of fish.

It wouldn't be the last time Carter made use of the *Rosa* and its captain, Arlev Guildenkov.

A knock on the door brought him back to the present.

*"Da."*

The door swung aside and she stood, hands on hips, with her shoulders and pelvis moving in all directions at once. She was far short of beautiful, but pretty, with a strikingly pale face surrounded by blue-black hair. The dress was cheap and tight everywhere, and she wore a tiny hat on her head set at a saucy angle.

"You want to see Ludmilla, comrade?" she said in a too-loud voice.

Carter nodded her in with a smile, and she closed and locked the door behind her.

"Can we talk?" he asked, rolling his eyes around the room.

She nodded. "They only put listening devices in the Intourist hotels down here."

"How much did he give you?" Carter asked.

"Ten rubles."

"The thief, I gave him thirty-five. Drink?"

"Yes. I've set up at meeting with Kokolev for tonight, ten o'clock."

"We'll stay in the room until then."

"Very well, then I can get rid of this for a while." She pulled off the black wig and shook out a radiant mane of honey-blond hair.

"Sorry I was late. I waited at the station until the train I was supposed to be on came in."

"That's all right," she said with a chuckle. "I was rather enjoying myself. Do you know I could have made over two hundred rubles this afternoon?"

Carter checked out of the room with the excuse that he had decided to leave for the south early.

Ludmilla had left an hour before him.

Carrying his suitcase, he walked to Ushakov Square and joined the line waiting for the bus. He could see the golden halo of her hair near the front of the line. She had discarded the cheap garb of the prostitute and now wore a severe dark suit, low-heeled shoes, and carried a huge shoulder bag.

Now she looked like what she really was: an Intourist guide.

It was a perfect cover for her real role as a courier. She would obtain documents or information from Moscow-based vacationing agents, and pass it along to her English or American tourist charges.

Her role as liaison/guide for Carter was dangerous and far out of her line, but the operation had to be mounted in a hurry.

The bus arrived and the long line filtered aboard. Carter sat near the rear, Ludmilla directly behind the driver. When she got off at the Mount Sapun stop, he followed her.

The night had grown chilly, but the narrow streets of the little village were full of walking, chatting people. Mount Sapun was cleaner and prettier than Sevastopol', with a lot of packed street cafés and basement bistros.

A light fog swirled around them as they drew closer to the sea. Ludmilla kept changing directions in a zigzag pattern,

THE BERLIN TARGET 7

and she even doubled back on herself twice. Carter knew she was checking for a tail, and went along.

When she halted at last, he continued walking until he caught her.

"It's not far now, just down the sea walk a little and then up to that row of houses—there."

Carter nodded and they set off.

Five minutes later, they had climbed to the seaward side of a long row of one-story, concrete-block houses.

"Go out on the point, there, and wait. It is best that his wife and children don't see you."

Carter nodded. They couldn't describe the face of a visitor they had never seen.

He moved out onto the overhanging cliff and hunkered down among the rocks. He scarcely had a cigarette going when Ludmilla appeared. She crouched opposite Carter, and then an enormous, black-haired man blocked out the moon before perching on a rock.

"I am Kokolev."

Carter nodded. He didn't give the man his own name. Kokolev knew what Carter was; there was no need of a who.

He cased the other man in the moonlight, and liked what he saw. Deep lines cut into the sides of his mouth. His flesh, roughened from exposure to sun, wind, and rain, was stretched taut over Tatar-like cheekbones, drawn tight over sunken cheeks. Under protruding black eyebrows, the pale blue eyes were intense as they studied Carter with equal care.

"Your target arrived in Sochi the day before yesterday."

"With the woman?"

"Yes. They are staying in a *dacha* at the compound near the Matsesta River, right on the sea. It is where all the very high government officials take their vacations."

"So it is very well guarded."

Kokolev nodded. "High, electrified fence three quarters of the way around, and patrols on the beach. Two of my cousins work there, so I know which house they are in."

"Do you have a plan?" Carter asked.

"Yes." Kokolev took a map from beneath his shirt and

spread it on the ground. A penlight appeared in his hand and danced over the paper.

"You have arranged for the fishing trawler to pick you up, correct?"

"Yes," Carter said and nodded. "All I need to know is exactly where we leave the coast. I can arrange coordinates then with Guildenkov. You have the undersea sleds I requested?"

"We do. They are old but in good repair." He returned to the map. "The workers' complex is here. That is where you and Ludmilla will check in tomorrow afternoon. It abuts the government officials' complex—here."

"From the sketch, it's practically a fortress," Carter commented.

"It is." Kokolev chuckled. "They wouldn't want outsiders, *real* workers, to wander into it and see how lavishly they live. The compound itself is enclosed, with two entrances, each guarded by a pair of sentries. Two more sentries act as a roving patrol, one on the beach side and one in the compound itself."

"Is this a complete floor plan of the *dacha*?"

"The woman who got it for me works in the Ministry of Engineering. It is the exact floor plan from which every building in the compound was built."

"Tricky," Carter growled. "We'll have to get rid of at least one set of guards at one of the entrances. Then, even after I'm inside, the two roving guards will have to be occupied for at least an hour."

"True," Kokolev replied. "And this is how I think it can be done."

For the next twenty minutes, the big man went over the plan, and Carter tried to tear it apart.

He couldn't. It looked solid.

"That means we'll need two men besides yourself, plus arms and uniforms."

"I have already procured all of those things," Ludmilla offered.

"And your two cousins? They will cooperate?"

"They have been softening up the guards for a week,"

Kokolev replied. "Actually, it was very easy. They are very jealous of the ones they stand watch over."

"It looks good. We'll go."

Kokolev nodded and smiled. "I have a delivery tomorrow near Soucha. I will take the two men and the equipment down in the truck. You and Ludmilla will take the ten o'clock bus. We will meet you at ten tomorrow night, here. Ludmilla . . ."

"I know the place."

Kokolev folded the sketch and handed it to Carter. "You will want to study this. Burn it before you leave in the morning."

Without another word, he stood and moved like a cat back toward the row of houses.

"This way," Ludmilla murmured to Carter, rising. "We will stay tonight in the house of Kokolev's brother. He and his wife have conveniently gone away for a few days. It is on the edge of the village."

"The neighbors . . ."

"We are two lovers from the north on vacation, and we do not dare check into a hotel together."

Carter nodded and grabbed his suitcase. He followed her down the cliffside, then paused on the ocean walk for a second.

"What are you thinking?"

"Just that this is a very dangerous game for all of you to play, with very little reward."

"Let us be the judge of that," Ludmilla replied quietly. "Besides, we are Tatars."

She moved away again, and the Killmaster fell in step behind her.

Tatars.

He knew exactly her meaning. Under the Soviets, in 1921, the Tatar Crimean Autonomous Republic was set up. They ruled themselves, and did it well. But during World War II, the Crimea was occupied by Germans for three years. This proved to have tragic consequences for the proud Tatars.

They were accused by Stalin of collaboration with the Nazis. All in all, this was not true. But it was a good excuse for the Soviet bear to swallow up the land at the end of the war and abolish self-rule.

The Crimean Tatar families were rounded up and banished to the Soviet republics in central Asia. Eventually, many of their offspring—like Ludmilla and Kokolev—returned, only to become bitter and disillusioned when they found themselves third-class citizens in their own land.

"Here we are," she said, opening the door.

The cottage was unimpressive from the outside, and even more so in the interior. It was stark and bare, with sagging, rugless wooden floors and Spartan furniture.

Light from a single coal-oil lamp illuminated a large room with a small wooden bed, a table and three chairs, and two sofas that had seen better days decades before. The kitchen was a tiny lean-to reached through an opening knocked through the original wall. An ancient tub sat in one corner with a pipe from its drain running through the wall. There were no pipes evident to run water into the tub.

Ludmilla saw his face as his gaze roamed around the room.

"These are very poor people. They cannot afford to live as you do in the West."

Carter smiled gently. "The West is not all a utopia, Ludmilla. There are poor people there, as well. I will take one of the sofas."

"There is no need," she replied calmly. "There is room for two in the bed."

Without waiting for a reply, she went in search of linen.

Carter found a bottle of vodka. He poured a glass for himself and held the bottle up to her. She shook her head, and shook out a sheet.

He sipped the strong liquid and watched her move around the bed. She had a long, lithe body, and she used it with an economy of movement.

"It's ready," she said at last, and extinguished the lamp.

He heard her shoes drop to the floor, and then she moved to the window. Her voice when she spoke seemed to be disembodied, as if the words weren't her own.

"It will be a clear, moonlit night tomorrow evening."

"Probably," Carter replied, discarding his own shoes.

"Are you frightened?"

"Yes. Why?"

"No reason," she murmured, shrugging out of her jacket. "I just wondered if people like you are ever afraid."

He stripped to his shorts and lay on one side of the bed. She hadn't moved from the window, and he could see, in the moonlight, her hands working on her own clothing.

Idly, Carter wondered if she were standing in the light on purpose, or if she was so lost in thought that she didn't realize that he could see every move she made.

Watching her undress, he found himself touched and affected by the naked slimness of her shoulders and her bare back. She had a beautiful back, but the shoulders were hunched slightly now.

"This man, this Boris Simonov . . . he must be very important to your people."

"He is."

She turned, poised in the shaft of flickering moonlight, immobile for an instant before moving to the bed. Ludmilla was not a woman of great physical beauty, but looking at the length of her nakedness, Carter felt a heavy sadness because she could so easily become beautiful.

He wasn't surprised when, as she slithered gently into the bed, she moved immediately to his side. She wriggled against him and eased one leg over his thighs.

"I thought tonight, for just a moment," she sighed, "how wonderful it would be to go with you."

"Would you like to?"

"No . . . not really."

She was silent. Then more movement, until one of his legs was captured between her thighs. He could feel her dampness as well as her softness.

He pulled her back against him. She came willingly and her long, smooth body pressed against his even longer, heavily muscled torso. He rubbed his hand up and down her back and lightly brushed his chin through the scented, golden halo of her hair. She smelled good and felt even better. His resolve not to get entangled began to weaken.

"I could never leave," she whispered. "Even though I am

a traitor, I am Russian.''

"Do you look upon yourself as a traitor?''

"Yes. Would you like to make love with me?''

"Yes.''

"I have very small breasts.''

"I hadn't noticed,'' he said, keeping the smile on his lips out of his voice.

"Good.''

Her hand moved through the mat of hair on his chest, down over his belly. Her fingers found the heavy pattern of scar tissue and stopped.

"What's that?''

"Something you'll never have.''

Lower, until her fingers found the elastic of his shorts.

It happened so quickly, it practically took his breath away. Her touch was deft, arousing him instantly. Suddenly she had rolled him above her and captured his hips with her straining thighs.

"There,'' she whispered, and her softness enveloped him.

# TWO

The bus ride was just under two hours. They both checked into the Soucha Workers' Recreation Center at a little past noon, Carter into the men's section, Ludmilla into the women's.

Carter thought there was some degree of irony in that, considering the very passionate lovemaking they had shared the night before. He thought it, but made a mental note to say nothing. That morning, before they had left separately for the bus that would take them south, Ludmilla had been cool and businesslike.

"When we arrive, do nothing out of the ordinary. Check in, unpack, and go about having a good time on the beach."

"Do you suppose it's all right if we have a chance meeting on the beach?"

She thought for a moment, and then nodded. "I should think so. This time of the year it will probably be a rather wild and drunken crowd. No one will remember seeing us together."

The bachelor cubicle he was assigned was spare but clean and contained all the essentials, and he shared a bath with only three other men. It wasn't exactly Club Med, he thought drily.

Doing as he was instructed, Carter unpacked and headed for the dining room. It was the lunch hour, and everyone else had the same idea. He got a plate of sandwiches and a large

13

mug of beer, and escaped the screaming children by moving into the communal lounge.

Modern sofas and chairs were grouped around glass-and-chrome tables under a large chandelier with small bright bulbs of clear glass. Along one wall a glistening Telefunken console blared a mixture of sad Russian music, rock'n'roll, and American pop songs from the 1940s and '50s.

Ludmilla sat with two women on one of the sofas, picking at food from a lap tray. The two women, one at each of her ears, chattered incessantly. One was a dumpy, matronly sort of about fifty, with a sharp expression in hard eyes glinting behind unflattering glasses. She shoveled food from the tray into her mouth as if she hadn't eaten since childhood. The other was tall, with a reed-thin body, pinched features, and severely cut hair.

Carter started to move toward them, but a warning look from Ludmilla's eyes stopped him. He moved away and found a window table for one.

When she got up to leave, her lips silently formed the words *Beach, one hour*.

Carter killed a half hour reading propaganda like a good party worker, then returned to his cubicle. He donned trunks, pulled on a sweat shirt to cover his scarred upper torso, took one of the issue towels, and hit the beach.

He baked, wiling away another half hour without looking for her. He figured she would find him. And she did.

She was working her way down the beach in a state of constant flirtation. And she had a lot to flirt with in the process.

She wore a scarlet cloth twisted around her head, turban fashion, and a scarlet knit top so tight-fitting that every hint of a curve on her sleek figure was shown to maximum effect. The sweater was high at the neck, and the sleeves stopped just above the elbows. She had slender, browned arms, her delicately shaped hands tipped with scarlet nail polish. The bikini bottom barely covered the essentials and left her long, tapering legs nicely bare to ogle.

It was a good gimmick. Every twenty-or-so yards, a single man jumped up to walk a few feet with her. None of them scored, but it fit for Carter to do the same when she hit his space.

"May I buy you a drink, comrade?"

"*Nyet*, comrade, but I would like a cigarette," she said with fluttering eyelashes and glossy lips.

He shook one from his pack, and they both cupped their hands over the match and her lips.

"We go early," she whispered.

"Why?"

"One of Kokolev's people got a message to me. They are checking out of the *dacha* at midnight. They have ordered a car."

"Then the woman has the information she wants."

"It would seem so. Eight o'clock, same place."

"Did Kokolev find out who the woman is?"

"Yes. The name isn't familiar to me . . . it's Anna Palmitkov." Her eyes darted up long enough to see the startled and then grim look on Carter's face. "You know her?"

"I know her."

"Eight o'clock," Ludmilla said, and walked away without questioning his sudden change of mood.

Carter flopped back on his towel and shielded the sun from his eyes with dark glasses and a forearm.

Ah, yes, he knew Anna Palmitkov. She was good, very good, a specialist on Germany. She had gone deep cover into Berlin several times. One of those times, Carter had gone up against her and her agent lover of the moment.

Carter had gotten the agent lover, but not Anna Palmitkov. In fact, the jagged, purplish scar that ran from his breastbone down to his right hip had been Anna's gift to him that time in Berlin.

No, he would never forget Anna Palmitkov.

A slight smile curved his lips as he relaxed and let the sun warm him.

It promised to be an interesting and exciting evening.

They checked out bicycles from the recreation pool fifteen minutes apart, and left the camp in separate directions. At precisely seven, they met again several miles down the beach.

"Anyone following?"

"No, I'm positive," Carter growled.

"Very well. I will lead."

Ludmilla led the way down to a lane that ran along the beach between the sand and the cliffs. Another two miles and she stopped. They hid the bicycles among the rocks and began to climb. Halfway up, she slipped into the mouth of a cave that Carter would have missed had he been alone.

"Back here!" came a guttural voice.

Carter stumbled after her, and then a hand grasped his. He was pulled into a low, cell-like stone room, and a candle was lit.

"Congratulations, you have arrived," Kokolev said, attempting the first bit of humor Carter had seen evidenced by the man.

"Where are we?" Carter asked.

"Three kilometers west of the compound line, and we will have to swim at least two kilometers out to sea in order to avoid the security nets. Here!"

Before pulling on the wet suit, Carter passed his papers to Ludmilla. She would change the photos, and Kokolev himself would ride the second bicycle back to the workers' compound and spend the night there as Mikhail Assalov.

Kokolev had already donned his own wet suit, the one that Boris Simonov would evidently wear. He had a silenced 9mm Makarov PM in a watertight oilskin holster strapped around him.

He handed its twin to Carter.

"Are your two men set?"

Kokolev nodded. "The party has already started in the guard room. As soon as the depressant takes effect, my two men, in uniform, will become the two-man roving patrol."

"How did they get in?"

"Earlier this afternoon in the garbage truck. Let us be off."

Kokolev extinguished the candle and moved into the night, with Carter behind him and Ludmilla bringing up the rear. At the mouth of the cave, she grasped his elbow. He turned, and she moved into his arms.

The kiss bespoke genuine warmth rather than passion. It was also short and to the point.

"Good-bye," she murmured, and moved away to climb an outcropping of rocks.

Carter watched her until she was gone. She was quite a lady, he thought, and moved on down to the beach.

"We go in here," Kokolev whispered.

Carter pulled on a set of flippers, adjusted his mask, and slipped into the water right behind the man.

They swam straight out for what seemed like an eternity before Kokolev made a left turn. Then they swam parallel to the shore for another fifteen minutes, until the man called a halt.

"We wait here!"

They treaded water for another fifteen minutes, and then a tiny flash from a penlight ashore told them that their own set of roving guards was in place.

As they started to swim ashore, Carter was thankful they had chosen the plan. A rock shelf lay beneath the water where they swam, making a calm mirror out of the bay.

A lone, unfriendly man on the beach with an AK-47 could spot them surfacing from a good distance. Add to it thirty yards of pure white, moonlit sand ashore, and they would be cut down in ten feet.

The moonlight knifing through the clear water created an eerie, ominous aura around them as they crawled out onto the sand.

They sprinted across the beach, thankful once again that no AK rifles were pointed their way. At a low stone wall they practically crashed into a uniformed man lounging against the stone, a rifle over his shoulder.

"It is a beautiful night," he grunted.

"They are still there?" Kokolev asked.

The man nodded. "The woman is in the *dacha*. The man has gone to the administration building, I would guess to sign the departure forms."

Carter slid the flippers from his feet, unzipped the holster, and vaulted over the wall. As he did so, he saw out of the corner of his eye Kokolev already climbing out of his wet suit and the uniform moving down the beach on the guards' usual rounds.

Bending low, Carter duck walked the width of two beach houses and dropped into the rear garden of the only one with lights glowing.

The air was sweet with blooming flowers and buzzing with insects. The only other sound as he wound his way through scrub and low citrus trees was a radio playing something maudlin from one of the nearby rooms.

He headed in that direction and carefully brought his eyes up over the window ledge.

He was just in time. It was the bedroom of the *dacha*, and Anna was just emerging from the bathroom, stark naked. He watched her pull on a pair of sheer panties and encase her voluptuous breasts in a lacy, very unproletariat bra.

Over that went a tight sweater and slim skirt, an outfit that should have made the hair on the back of his neck and inner thighs tingle.

It didn't.

It made the scar across his chest itch and ache.

He scanned the room. A half-packed suitcase lay open on the bed. Two closed cases sat by the door. He couldn't see a phone, and there was no sign of a weapon.

Anna went to work on her dark hair, and Carter took a turn around the whole house. He ended up back at the sliding glass doors that led from the garden into a large sitting room.

The room and its decor was about as far removed from the hovel where he and Ludmilla had spent the night as Washington was from Moscow.

The party elite and their favored people didn't suffer.

The room was done well, in soft tones, and the furniture was modern and expensive. Chrome-framed prints and antique tapestries somehow worked together on the walls. The prints were French Impressionist paintings and, strangely enough, were mostly Renoir nudes.

The sliding doors opened easily, and he moved into the room. He finally located the phone and cut the cord. When the intercom on the wall was jammed, he moved to a well-stocked portable bar.

It was foolish, he thought, but something deep inside him made him want to handle it this way.

He sloshed vodka into a glass, unholstered the Makarov, and sat down to wait.

It wasn't long. She glided into the room, still brushing her hair, and came up short with a gasp six feet from where he sat.

She was even more beautiful and arresting from the front than she had been from the rear. And, up close, the tight-fitting clothes left little to the imagination.

"You! How . . .?"

"Good evening, Anna," Carter said, saluting her with the glass and the long snout of the Makarov's silencer.

It hit her hard, but it took only seconds for her to regain composure.

She was a cool cookie, he thought, like ice, as she tossed her hair from her face and took in the pistol and wet suit at a glance. The hard, dark eyes finally settled on his. They spoke challenge, and he answered it.

"Submarine?" she growled.

"In the Black Sea? Of course not. This is your turf. That would be far too dangerous. But I did emerge from the sea like a nymph."

She started to turn toward the bedroom, her strong thighs moving steadily, lushly visible under the skirt. They stopped moving when Carter put a slug into the doorjamb two inches from her shoulder.

If she was unnerved when she turned back to face him, she didn't show it. But her mind was obviously working, and her eyes were darting from Carter to the glass doors.

"Go ahead," he said. "But I wouldn't advise it. Your guards aren't there. Mine are."

She shrugged, then moved to the bar. "I should have made sure you were dead in Berlin."

"Yes, you should have."

"You are a clever, dangerous, and resourceful man."

"Yes, I am."

She poured a drink and walked past him to the opposite sofa. She rolled her long legs under her like a cat. When she spoke again, she also purred like one.

"You've come for Boris."

Carter nodded. "Why go through all this to get what he knows? Why not just use a needle?"

"Two reasons," she replied in a bored voice, "and you should know both of them. We routinely, daily, take antidotes to combat truth chemicals . . . yours. Unfortunately, they also contradict our own drugs. There wasn't time to hospitalize Boris until the chemicals would work."

"And the second reason?"

"We were not positive that he had turned." She sipped her drink and smiled. The smile was far from warm and friendly, but it did fantastic things to the fine bones of her face. "We are now."

"*Touché*," Carter replied, smiling himself.

"Boris is a spineless jackass, but he works well in the West. He also has a genius for organization."

"An organization that you are now completely aware of."

"Perhaps." Her eyes came up, mirroring the vacant coldness of his own. "You managed somehow to get in here, but you'll never get out, not two of you. And, besides, I'm not so sure Boris will go with you . . . now."

"I think he will. You're very beautiful, Anna, but not beautiful enough to die for."

The door opened, slammed, and Boris Simonov emerged from the alcove and walked into the room behind Anna. He was tall and spare, with a weak chin. His dishwater-gray eyes grew wide with shock when he saw the tableau before him.

"Who . . ."

"Hello, Boris. Or I imagine I should call you Peter, since I've come to get you out."

"How did you . . ."

Anna slid off the sofa and slithered to his side. Possessively, she curled her arms around one of his.

"His name is Nicholas Carter," she said. "He's a one-man American assassination team, and he's probably come to kill you."

Simonov went even paler and shifted his eyes from Carter to the woman and back again.

"Let me give it to you straight, Boris," Carter growled, getting to his feet and making sure the barrel of the Makarov was trained solely on the woman. "They found out that we turned you. That's why you were called back. This 'wife' you were supposed to acquire was only meant to get what's in your head so that another deep-cover agent could go in and take up where you left off."

"Preposterous!" Anna said, and tugged harder, trying to keep him against her.

It didn't work. Simonov was already backing away from her, his face a chalky white and his body shaking in fright.

"It's true, Boris. Anna was supposed to get everything out of you she could, and then you were on your way back to Moscow. Where were you headed when you left here to-night, Boris?"

"Moscow," he stammered.

"And from there it was a gulag, at best. At the worst . . ." Carter shrugged, leaving Simonov to fill in the inevit-able.

"It's true, isn't it?" the frightened man said, staring at the woman he had probably been making love to the past two nights. "Isn't it?"

Anna knew she'd been unmasked. The Killmaster could see it in her eyes.

Carter thought, wrongly, that she would go for him. Anna was too much the trained agent. Instead of Carter, she went for Simonov. If the Russians couldn't retain what he had accomplished in the West, then the Americans wouldn't have it either.

She was like a panther, fast and sharp. In a split second she had the narrow chain belt from her waist around Simonov's throat. Her hands were trained, skilled in killing.

Simonov was no match for her, and Carter couldn't get in a shot without hitting him. The belt became a garrote, and her knee in the small of his back was doing the rest of the work.

Carter had only seconds, and he used them.

It was useless to try and flank her. Everywhere the

Killmaster approached, she turned Simonov's body to head him off.

Finally he gave up and plowed into both of them. His shoulder hit Simonov in the gut, driving the wind from him and slamming Anna into the wall.

The long barrel of the Makarov cracking across one of her wrists brought enough slack in the belt to allow Carter's fingers to get between it and the man's neck.

When Carter pulled it away, Simonov fell to the floor gagging. Anna recovered instantly, even though it was obvious that her right wrist was broken. With the fingers of her left hand curled, she went for Carter's throat.

He barely avoided a death blow to his windpipe by spinning and taking the blow on his ear. Bells rang and he was staggered, but he managed to continue the spin and drive his knee into her belly.

As she doubled over, he brought the long-barreled silencer down across the back of her neck.

She had scarcely crumpled to the floor before Carter was on her, the tip of the Makarov nuzzled just behind her left ear.

He was just squeezing, when Simonov lurched and dragged Carter's arm to the side. The powerful gun popped, but the slug dug harmlessly into the carpet.

"Damn you!" Carter hissed, backing the man across the room with a shoulder to Simonov's belly.

"No!" Simonov gasped, holding his aching gut with both hands and looking as though all he wanted to do in the world was vomit. "No, don't kill her!"

"Why not!" Carter moved the Makarov back to the woman's skull.

"No!" Boris shouted in the loudest voice he could muster, and staggered again toward the Killmaster.

"You damned fool! She almost killed me once, and she would have had you killed within the next three or four days!"

"No . . . please. I'll go with you, do anything your people want me to, but don't kill her . . ."

Carter looked at the pain in the man's contorted face, then down at the beautiful woman on the floor.

Obviously Boris Simonov was a normal man, subject to the emotions and passions of a normal man.

"How much have you told her?"

"Nothing of consequence, I swear it!" Simonov replied, jabbering wildly. "I swear it! I guessed what they were doing. I told her that I put everything in a report and that it was in my Moscow apartment. That was why we were leaving tonight. It was my insurance."

"What were you going to do once you got to Moscow?"

His eyes fell. "I hadn't figured that out yet."

"Figures," Carter growled. "If you're lying, Simonov, you know you're of little use to us. If she knows what you know, we'll give you right back to them."

"She doesn't, I swear it! She knows a little, yes. Bits and pieces I told her to bring her on, get her trust . . . but only a few things. Don't kill her, Carter, please."

*You poor fool*, Carter thought, but he hauled the woman to her feet. Then he slid his arm under her shapely rear end, lifted her high in the air, and started for the bedroom.

"What . . . what are you doing?"

"I've got to do something with her—I can't just leave her lying in here. She's already waking up. Simonov . . ."

"Yes?"

"Get back up to the administration office. Explain that you and she have changed your minds. Got that?"

"Yes . . . yes."

"Have them change the order for your car to seven in the morning. Have them change your reservations to Moscow accordingly. Understand?"

"Yes."

"When you return, don't even bother coming in here. Go to the beach, over the wall. There's a man there with a wet suit. Get it on and be ready to go when I get there."

"I'll do it."

"You'd better."

Simonov started walking to the door, then paused and turned. "Carter . . ."

"Yeah?"

"You promise?"

"I promise."

"As a gentleman?"

"Look, Boris, I'm a long way from being a fucking gentleman, but you've got my word that she'll be alive when I leave here."

The Russian scooted out the door, and Carter continued on into the bedroom. Unceremoniously he dumped Anna on the bed and searched in the open suitcase for panty hose. By the time her eyes were blinking and she was shaking herself awake, both of her arms and her legs were tied securely to the four-poster.

"Bastard, you've broken my neck!" she groaned.

"You're lucky that's all," Carter said.

A string of Russian curses that even Carter didn't know erupted from her mouth as he rummaged again in the bag.

"You had better kill me, bastard, because if we ever meet again, I'll kill you . . . and as slowly as I can."

"You know something?" he said, pausing in his search. "I believe you. The only reason I'm not putting a needle in your arm is to keep Simonov happy."

She started to scream another series of oaths at him, but it ended abruptly when Carter rolled a pair of panties into a ball and stuffed them into her mouth.

Using a scarf from the bag, he secured the gag in her mouth and then stood staring down at her. "Stay over here, Anna. Don't come to the West again. If you do, I'll hunt you down like the viper you are."

Her eyes flashed pure hatred in reply as Carter went around the room closing drapes and shutting off lights. He did the same in the living room, then let himself out into the garden.

Kokolev waited with Simonov and the two phony Russian guards. Both of them had already shed their uniform tunics and their rifles for the swim. Simonov had pulled on the wet suit.

"All right, let's go!"

"Carter," Simonov stammered, "is she . . ."

"She's alive," Carter growled. "But she won't be if I ever see her again."

The four of them slid into the water. They retraced the

swim that Carter and Kokolev had made earlier.

Ludmilla was waiting. She had dragged the powered sleds down to the beach.

Just before pushing off, Carter turned to Kokolev. "If you, or she . . . or any of you people ever want out—"

Kokolev interrupted him with a raised hand. "We won't."

The Killmaster nodded in understanding. He shook the big man's hand and glanced at Ludmilla. "Good luck," he said gently. Then he turned to the Russian. "C'mon, Boris!"

Two hours later they abandoned the sleds and hoisted themselves over the rail of the *Rosa*.

# THREE

Lisa Berrington's beautiful, usually soft features were set in hard lines as she tooled the little sports car across the Key Bridge from Arlington. Once over the bridge she turned right, onto the Whitehurst Freeway, and took the Wisconsin Avenue turnoff into the heart of Georgetown.

Her dark blond hair glinted in the sun as the wind swirled it about her shoulders. Her blue eyes and delicate features concentrated on the traffic around her, but a close observer would have noticed that her mind was absorbed with more than her driving.

Lisa was beautiful in a refined, classic way. She came from an old, aristocratic Virginia family, and there was nothing brassy or coarse about her, even though, no matter what she wore, her figure turned heads wherever she went.

Now she wore a simple navy skirt, a mint-green sweater set, and a navy and white scarf was draped around her neck. It was hardly the outfit she would have chosen for that day, but she had been in a hurry to leave her apartment when Ginger Bateman had agreed to meet her.

Ginger was not exactly an old friend, but because Lisa had been involved with a couple of AXE-related jobs, she knew the head of that agency's secretary and right hand fairly well.

Lisa hoped she knew Ginger well enough. She realized that the request she was about to make of the woman was pretty bizarre.

She handled the powerful little sports car with precision, driving aggressively and knowledgeably, right hand on the shift, long legs scissoring over gas, brake, and clutch with agility.

In the drive of the Pierre, a popular Georgetown restaurant, she left the motor running and accepted the attendant's hand. The car roared away into the parking lot as Lisa entered the building.

"A table for one, mademoiselle?"

"No, I'm meeting someone . . . a Miss Bateman."

"Ah, yes. Right this way."

The interior decor was a pleasing mixture of expensive leather, high ceilings and windows, elegant draperies, and lots of greenery.

The maître d' guided her toward a table for two in one of the smaller dining rooms. They were halfway there when Lisa spotted Ginger Bateman's glossy black hair and tall figure.

The woman looked up and smiled. Lisa returned the smile as she slid into the opposite chair.

"Good to see you again."

"Thank you," Lisa replied. "It's been a long time."

"Would mademoiselle care for a drink?"

"One of those will be fine," Lisa said, nodding toward the concoction sitting in front of Ginger.

The maître d' glided away, and Ginger leaned forward, lowering her voice. "How's Langley?"

"Unchanged. I've been upgraded. I'm a courier now."

"Congratulations."

Neither woman voiced what their eyes were communicating. AXE had borrowed Lisa twice from the CIA for delicate missions. The second time she had almost been killed. Afterward, when she had been returned to the Company, she had been reclassified away from field agent status.

It had hurt, but Lisa had accepted it. Her superiors had feared that she had lost her nerve. Lisa feared the same thing, so she had accepted "white" work and a desk.

Being put on courier duty was a big step back up for her.

The drink came, and the two women saluted each other with their glasses.

"I must say I was a little surprised to get your call," Ginger said, studying the other woman over the rim of her glass.

"Yes, I suppose you were. I need a favor, Ginger . . . a big one."

"I'll do what I can."

"I need to get in touch with Nick Carter."

Bateman's face turned to stone. Her hard eyes stopped any further mention of AXE's top agent.

"I suggest that we have lunch and then take a drive around beautiful Georgetown."

Lisa nodded. "That might be a good idea."

"Shall we order? The name is French, but they have marvelous German dishes," Ginger said, replastering a smile on her face.

They both ordered a breaded veal cutlet topped with a fried egg and served with fresh vegetables. Ginger mentioned wine, but Lisa demurred, suggesting Perrier instead.

They ate sparingly, moving through the meal with offhand chatter about the mounting costs of living in the nation's capital and the ludicrousness of the latest youth-oriented fashions.

Ginger could see that her luncheon companion was getting increasingly nervous with each passing minute. She passed on dessert and requested the check.

"Let me . . ." Lisa protested.

"No, I'll put it on the account," Ginger replied with a wave of a hand. "After all, it does look like we're going to be discussing business."

She paid the check and they moved through the front doors.

"What are you driving?"

"An Alfa," Lisa replied. "Convertible."

"We'll take mine. I'll drive . . . you talk."

Ginger handed the attendant her car claim check, and five minutes later they pulled out of the parking lot and headed north past the Naval Observatory and toward Chevy Chase.

"Is Nick in the States?"

"You know I can't tell you that."

"I have his home number. I called it all night long and this morning. There was no answer."

Ginger knew that Carter and this woman had worked together. One look at Lisa Berrington's face and figure told her why she had the number of Carter's Georgetown condo.

"He's not in the country right now, Lisa. You know that's all I can tell you until you tell me more."

"I know," Lisa sighed. "Do you know my sister, Delaine?"

Ginger chuckled. "I know *of* her. I've seen her picture in the paper a few hundred times. I don't travel in those circles."

"But you do know her husband, Stephan Conway."

"Yes, I know about him."

Lisa smiled and met Ginger's eyes. "File?"

Ginger nodded. There was no need to say more. The CIA and the FBI both had extensive files on Stephan Conway. AXE also held a copy of those files as a matter of course.

Stephan Conway was quite a man, or character, depending on which side of him a person stood.

He had been a youthful computer genius and a student activist in the sixties. He eventually lost his rebellious nature, abandoned his liberal activism, and founded a small computer electronics company, Protec, that grew and grew until Conway was a rich man, even by Silicon Valley standards.

But for him that wasn't enough. With the power and wealth that came with his marriage to Delaine Berrington, he went after huge government contracts . . . and got them. He began buying up small companies and merging with larger ones all over the world, with himself always retaining controlling interest.

By the early 1980s, the company was the undisputed leader in its field, and the government's chief supplier of electronic radar and missile guidance systems.

This knowledge of modern technology, coupled with his

wealth, his worldwide business interests, and the enormous clout of his Washington contacts, had recently shoved Stephan Conway into the political arena.

It was an unannounced fact that he would run for a Senate seat in the upcoming elections.

"I got a call from Delaine last night, from West Berlin."

"Yes?"

"It's driving me out of my mind," Lisa blurted.

"How so?"

"Two reasons, really. First, Stephan himself. As you probably know, our parents left both of us very well off. I have always thought that Stephan married Delaine solely for our family name and contacts and her wealth."

"And now the marriage is going sour?" Ginger asked drily.

"I think it's been going sour right from the beginning, and Delaine is just realizing it. She not only sounded very down on the phone, she also sounded scared . . . petrified."

Ginger pulled into one of the narrow, tree-shaded streets of Chevy Chase, cruised for another half block, and pulled to the curb.

"Afraid?" she asked when she had killed the engine.

"Yes, very."

"I hate to say this, Lisa, but why Nick? I mean, he's hardly trained to handle domestic squabbles."

"I know that," Lisa replied, her face flushing slightly. "There's something else. Delaine hinted that some friends had shown up from Stephan's past. It happened a few weeks ago in California. There was a terrible fight, and when Delaine approached him about it, he called them 'blackmailing bastards' and said that he had told them to go to hell."

"But that wasn't the end of it?"

"No," Lisa replied. "At least, Delaine doesn't think so. Stephan became more and more nervous. And he began to lock himself in his study late at night and make all sorts of odd phone calls. And when they started on this speaking tour in Europe, he hired four bodyguards."

"Speaking tour?"

"Yes, he's going to five countries for the State Department. He's speaking to rallies, trying to convince them of the wisdom and the safety of the NATO missiles."

"I see," Ginger sighed. "That alone would give him reason to hire bodyguards."

"Yes, I suppose it would. But the last thing Delaine said really shook me up. Last night, just before her phone call, they were at a dinner party with a group of German dignitaries, and Delaine overheard Stephen tell two high-ranking German officials that he was positive there was a plot to assassinate him."

This brought Ginger out of her slouch. "Well, that puts a different light on the matter. But Nick . . .?"

"I didn't want to go to anyone in the Company. I was afraid they would think I was crazy, especially since Stephan and Delaine do have a domestic problem. And besides, I do know Nick personally, and I know what he's capable of accomplishing. Dammit, Ginger, if you would just speak to your boss . . ."

Ginger furrowed her brow and pursed her lips in thought. She had a pretty good idea that David Hawk would either laugh until his sides hurt, or explode in anger at the idea of his top operative running off to settle a future senator's domestic problems.

On the other hand, if Stephan Conway were being blackmailed and threatened, it could be a major security bomb.

There was also Lisa herself to consider. She was a highly intelligent woman, familiar with the realities of the espionage game, and normally level-headed and rational, certainly not prone to hysteria. Now her nerves were obviously frayed at the ends, and she apparently firmly believed that everything her sister feared had a basis in fact. If she was this shaken, it warranted at least a cursory investigation.

"I'll tell you what, Lisa. I can't promise much, but I'll do what I can."

"When?"

"First thing in the morning."

"Can't you speak to him this afternoon, or this evening?"

"It's Sunday, and I'm not sure he's even in town," Ginger replied.

And, she thought, even if he were—and agreed to let Carter help—where *was* N3?

He had gotten Boris Simonov to Istanbul, and the last thing Ginger had heard, they were readying false papers to get him on to England or Paris for interrogation.

"I promised Delaine I would get the first flight out to Frankfurt and then on to Berlin. I'm leaving tonight. If I could, I'd like to know something before I leave."

Ginger shrugged and started the car. "As I said, I'll do what I can."

She drove to Connecticut Avenue and turned south. In minutes they had passed out of Montgomery County and entered the District of Columbia.

Ginger pulled the car over when she spotted a corner phone booth.

"Sit tight."

Lisa nervously chewed on her lip and worried the small purse in her lap as she concentrated on Ginger's face through the clear sides of the booth.

The phone call seemed to go on for an eternity.

When at last Ginger returned, Lisa could feel perspiration flowing down her back, making her sweater stick to her skin.

"You're in luck. He'll see you. But beyond that, who knows?"

"I'll be convincing," Lisa replied with a sigh.


She took great care building his drink, and when she finished, she stood facing him at the bar. There was something special in the way she looked at him. Her eyes dimmed, becoming smoky behind the long lashes, and her full breasts brought a catch in his throat as she took a lazy breath.

"You're afraid."

"Aren't you?" he replied.

"It is too late for fear now, my darling."

She came across the room toward him, tucking the blouse into her skirt with her free hand, making it taut over the lush curves.

"Could I have a cigarette?" she asked, handing him the drink.

He held out the pack, and she plucked a cigarette from it with long, crimson-tipped fingers. She put the filter tip between equally red lips and leaned over toward the flame.

The front of her blouse fell open, and his eyes slid into the deep darkness between her breasts.

His lip quivered and his mouth went dry.

"He is set," she said, looking up at him with bold, appraising eyes. "Half of the money has been delivered. I have already arranged for the other half. He has the equipment. Believe me, darling, it will soon be over."

She tugged him to his feet. She was standing so close that he could feel the faint touch of her breasts on his chest and the heat of her breath on his neck.

"You're shaking, darling."

He was, and he knew it. But now he didn't know if it was from fear of what they were about to do, or the nearness of her body.

"Come, darling . . . into the bedroom."

She tugged on his arm and he followed her like a robot. As he neared the bed, the fog of desire momentarily left his brain.

"I shouldn't . . . they'll be waiting . . ."

"Darling, after tomorrow it will be a long time . . . this may be our last time for a long while."

Slowly she unbuttoned the blouse and revealed the naked body beneath it. Then, deftly, she freed the zipper on the skirt and shrugged, the garments puddling at her feet.

"God," he gasped, "you're so beautiful."

Her breasts were heavy, yet firm and high, creamy white with coral tips that gleamed like beacons of desire. Her shoulders were firm and wide, yet capable of turning to melted butter when the right man put his arms around them. Her ribs poked excitingly against the flawless skin below her breasts, pointing like arrows to her navel, and below.

"Tomorrow," he moaned, stripping the clothing from his own body. "Tomorrow it will all be over."

She oozed back onto the bed and he fell between her legs.

"No, my darling, tomorrow it will just be starting . . . for us."


Carter fixed a scotch neat and moved to the hotel balcony. The drizzle that had shrouded Paris for the last forty-eight hours had lifted. Now the lights of the city blinked invitingly under a clear, starry sky.

Carter was weary. It had been a long day. But he was also itchy. It had been a good mission, and it had gone well, but he remembered Ludmilla, and for the last few hours he had been wondering how long she would last.

He needed to get her out of his mind.

In the distance he could see the lights of Montmartre and the gleaming dome of Sacré Coeur.

He knew a couple of little cafés around the square up there where he could easily find someone who would chase the thoughts of Ludmilla from his mind. He finished his drink and slipped a tie under his collar. The knot was barely adjusted when the telephone jangled.

"Yeah?"

"Nick, Carpenter at the office."

"Yes?"

"Home calling. They would like you to buzz them back from here."

"I'll be right there."

He cursed, shrugged into his jacket, and went downstairs. It took fifteen minutes to reach the Amalgamated Press and Wire Services offices.

Inside, he punched the proper code into a rear elevator that whisked him to the top floor and the real offices: AXE, Paris branch.

Hal Carpenter waved to him as he entered the computer room. "Use line three on the scrambler phone. It's already open all the way through."

"To whom?"

"To the old man himself."

"Oh, Christ," Carter growled, "there goes my week's vacation."

"Seven-four-seven."

"Ginger, Nick here. What's up?"

"That was quick."

"I'm a slave to command."

"I'll put you through."

Carter waited, and then the gruff, cigar-ruined voice boomed across the sea and half of France. "N3, good job . . . congratulations."

"Thank you, sir."

"How did the interrogation go?"

"Fine. We have all the contacts, routes, and most of the greedy bastards in the States who were ready to sell. Simonov has agreed to go hot again until the stateside boys can set up a sting."

"Good enough. Where is he now?"

"On his way to London. The MI6 people want to have a go at him tonight. Our boys will fly him out to Andrews in the morning."

"That's what I like," David Hawk said and chuckled. "A neat package. I checked with Alma Control about an hour ago. You asked for a few days."

"Yes, sir. Thought I'd hit Nice, get some sun. Is it off?"

"Not exactly. Remember Lisa Berrington?"

It only took two clicks of his memory bank. "I remember."

"She's got a problem. It's personal, wants to talk to you."

"But she's already talked to you."

"Yes. It's nothing we can do anything about, but we do owe her something."

"Yes, we do," Carter replied, remembering how the woman had looked on the floor of a Hong Kong hotel room with a bullet in her.

It had been an easy mission. No one should have gotten hurt. Lisa Berrington had almost bought the farm.

"I really can't authorize anything, and I won't. But if, after you talk to her, you want to check it out, you can. You're on vacation for a week."

Carter thought of all the beautiful, braless bodies on the pebbly beaches of Nice, and the equally lovely scenery not far away at Cannes and St.-Tropez.

Then he thought of Lisa Berrington.

"You still there, N3?"

"Yeah, I'm still here. You have a number?"

Hawk gave him a stateside number in Alexandria just outside Washington, and he signed off.

"Carpenter?"

"Yeah, Nick?"

"You got anything to drink around here?"

"You know that's against company policy, Nick."

"I didn't ask you about company policy."

"Last drawer down on your right."

It was a cheap brand that Carter hated, but at that point, in that place, it was any port in a storm. At that, it was better than the vodka he'd been slugging down not too many days before.

He poured three fingers in a foggy glass and dialed.

"Hello?"

The voice wasn't recognizable through the distortion on the scrambler line. "Lisa Berrington?"

"Yes."

"Lisa, this is Nick Carter."

"Oh, thank God . . ."

"I just talked to Washington. I hear you have a problem."

"Lots."

She launched into it, and hardly put a comma or a period in until she was finished. He had wiped out the three fingers by the time she finally wound down.

"That's it in the proverbial nutshell. Not much, huh?"

"I'm afraid not. Why me, Lisa?"

He swore he could hear her swallow hard before she spoke again. "Because you're so damned efficient . . . and you seem to know so many people all over the world . . . and Delaine sounded so frightened. . . . I thought you might be able to talk to Stephan and poke around . . ."

"Whoa, hold it, hold it . . . slow down, darlin'."

"And if there is anything wrong, I guess I figure you can work miracles. Ginger said you were in Europe. She didn't say where."

Carter thought for a moment, and decided that it didn't

matter . . . now. "I'm in Paris. You said you were coming over?"

"Yes. I'm on Pan Am out of Kennedy at nine forty-five tonight. I was just leaving the apartment to catch the shuttle at National when you called."

"Frankfurt?"

"Yes, with one stop in London. My flight gets into Frankfurt at ten-thirty. I change planes there and arrive in Berlin at one-thirty. Stephan is speaking to an antinuclear convention at one, so I told Delaine I would meet her at the hotel at three."

"All right. What's your Berlin flight number?"

"Nine-two-two."

"I'll be on it."

"Thank you, Nick, so much."

"But if nothing's up, I demand four days of wild night life in Berlin."

"You've got it," she said, managing a laugh at last.

"See you."

"Until tomorrow, then. And thank you again, Nick," she replied, and the line went dead.

"Carpenter!"

"Jesus, Nick, what is it now? I've got four more reports to file before I can eat, and it's almost midnight already."

"Sorry, old buddy. Can you get me out of here to Frankfurt in the morning in time to catch Flight Nine-two-two Pan Am into Berlin?"

"Hold on, I'll check."

Carter sipped another scotch. Minutes later, Carpenter was back.

"You're set. I'll have the tickets messengered to your hotel early tomorrow morning. They'll be at the desk. Is that it?"

"That's it."

"What's in Berlin?"

"An old flame," Carter said, and walked out into the Paris night, all thoughts of the two cafés in Montmartre pushed from his mind.

# FOUR

Fräulein Gertrude Klammer held her right wrist with her left to stop it from shaking as she applied lipstick to her thin lips.

She was rather pretty, in a stern, aging way, with light brown hair that she always wore pulled into a severe bun at the back of her head. The skirt and full blouse she wore were just as severe. Over the blouse she wore a baggy cardigan sweater. She had the nervous habit of pulling the cardigan together, as if her primness could hide her quite remarkable figure.

The severity and the primness were acquired characteristics. The remarkable figure had been acquired at the age of twelve, and it was on it that she blamed most of her troubled life.

From the age of thirteen, men had been attracted to Gertrude, and she found it impossible to resist them. And all she ever got from men was a child . . . and a police record from the prostitution and petty thievery she had engaged in to feed her son.

Now the boy was seventeen and was enrolled in the Hauptdort Academy in Leipzig. He was a gentleman, and he didn't know that his mother ran a back-street dive that catered to pimps and whores, and a small hotel above it that charged for its rooms by the hour.

It was a good job, reliable and secure, even though it did

not pay well enough. And for that reason, Gertrude was not above doing a little moonlighting now and then.

The messages, always folded around a five-hundred-mark note, had started arriving three weeks before. It wasn't the first time her mysterious employer had requested her services in such a way.

There were three altogether, simple and typewritten on plain paper and slipped under her door.

*We will be requiring your services very soon*, read the first one.

A week later the second arrived: *A white Mercedes sedan has been reserved for you at Europa car rental. Claim the car at Tegel Airport on Friday afternoon at three o'clock sharp.*

Gertrude had picked up the car and returned to the hotel, where she had parked it in an all-night garage just off the Kurfürsten Damm nearby.

She had awakened that Sunday morning in a cold sweat, and it got worse when she spotted the white envelope by her front door.

The message was much longer, but equally as terse in its demands. There was also a key in the envelope.

> *Tonight, at exactly midnight, you will deliver the car to Number 9 Wiebe Strasse. It is off Moabit Allee in the south of the Wedding section. The house is vacant. The key is to the padlock on the garage door. Park the car inside and leave the padlock key and the car keys on the seat. Beneath two bricks to your left of the door is one half of your bonus, 1000 marks. Lock the door when you leave.*
>
> *You will receive another message on Tuesday telling you where to pick up the car. When you deliver it back to Tegel, the deposit will be delivered to you in cash. You may keep it as the rest of your bonus.*
>
> *Needless to say, Fräulein Klammer, you never received any of these messages.*

Fräulein Klammer adjusted her sweater, grabbed a purse,

and left her top-floor apartment. Halfway down the stairs, she ran into the night chambermaid.

"*Guten Tag, Fräulein Klammer*," the old woman said, ambling on by her, shoulders bent forward with the load of linen she carried.

"And good morning to you, Marie. Busy?"

"*Ja, ja . . .* such sin on the sabbath! This is what we have come to!"

Marie was right. The desk on the floor above the street was crowded. Four girls were standing in line waiting for room keys. Their customers stood shyly in the shadows against the far wall.

"Georg?"

"*Ja, Fräulein?*"

"I'm going out for a while. I shouldn't be over an hour or so."

"*Ja, ja.*"

She looked into the hotel bar on the street floor. It was crowded, and the air was filled with deafening American rock music as well as the scent of stale beer and cloying, cheap perfume. Holding her breath and pulling her sweater together as she always did, she moved through the smoky room and stepped out onto Roscher Strasse.

To her left, the night sounds of the Ku'Damm blasted at her. She moved quickly toward the sound and the garish neons. Once on the Ku'Damm, she walked past peep shows, all-night strip clubs, and sex movies to the garage.

*I know nothing,* she thought as she climbed behind the wheel of the Mercedes. *I am guilty of nothing but picking up the car and taking it back. What it is used for has nothing to do with me. I am guilty of nothing.*

But as Fräulein Gertrude Klammer pulled out onto the Ku'Damm and turned north toward the Wedding section of West Berlin, she vowed that this would be the last time she would accept one of the envelopes and its shady commands.

Dieter Klauswitz throttled the big, powerful BMW back and leaned it left. Skillfully he eluded oncoming traffic on the

See Strasse and glided into the Volkspark Rehberge.

Ahead of him stretched the wide motorway that split the park from east to west. To his right was the Plotzensee. About a hundred yards inside the entrance he darted the powerful motorcycle into the trees onto a pedestrian walk and bicycle lane.

There were several strollers who dodged out of his way, but none of them screamed abuses at him. Pedestrians were used to the ill-mannered long-haired youths who rode their powerful machines anywhere they chose.

They only shook their heads and continued their evening stroll as Klauswitz roared around the lake.

But beneath the black leather and helmet with its dark visor was no raw youth with long hair and greasy beard.

Dieter Klauswitz was clean-shaven with cold, intense blue eyes and chiseled Aryan features. His hair was strikingly blond and carefully trimmed. And beneath the leather jacket and leather pants was a toned and athletic body.

Dieter Klauswitz was thirty-eight years old, and an accomplished thief.

As a youth he had honed his body to perfection. His desire, while he was growing up in Bavaria, was to be a great downhill skier.

That had failed.

In place of it he had trained himself in the cross-country biathlon. He schooled himself on every make of rifle known to man and became an expert. His instructors eventually deemed him one of the best marksmen they had ever seen. They also deemed him one of the worst skiers.

And Klauswitz had another flaw. He loved nice things . . . clothes, food, the best wines, the most beautiful women.

He became a thief, and a good one. His athletic body allowed him to scale walls like a human fly, and his alert mind and nimble fingers enabled him to open safes whenever he chose.

But Klauswitz got caught. He went to prison, was released, and got caught again.

Now he was awaiting trial, and his old ability with a rifle

was going to save him. He had no compunction about killing someone, anyone, if he could secure a new identity, a great deal of money, and avoid another prison term.

That was why he was in the Volkspark Rehberge, and doing business with Herr Oskar Hessling.

At the westernmost part of the park was a walled cemetery. The walkway ended abruptly in the trees that separated the lake from the cemetery.

Klauswitz drove the BMW off into the trees until he was completely enshrouded in darkness. He killed the engine and sat for several seconds. When he was sure no one had seen and become curious about his maneuver, he put the bike on its stand and moved soundlessly through the trees.

With ease he vaulted the stone wall and moved like a specter through the tombstones. It was difficult reading the names and the dates on the markers through the dark visor before his face, but he dared not raise it. The last thing he wanted was for the Turk to see his face.

"He always delivers," Hessling had said. "He doesn't know me; he mustn't know you. He will hand over the goods; you will hand over the envelope. You will never see each other again."

Klauswitz had to hand it to Oskar Hessling. He was a planner. He planned everything down to the last detail. Nothing was left to go astray.

That was why Klauswitz had agreed to perform this service for the man. That and, of course, the fringe benefits.

When, deep in the cemetery, it became just too dark to make his way, he used a small penlight.

At last he found it: KRONER LANE, PLOTS 16–34.

He had barely snapped off the light when a short, dark figure in jeans and a dark jacket materialized from nowhere.

"Good evening, *effendi*."

"You are the Turk?"

"I am."

"Frau Horning is buried near here."

"I believe she is in Number Eighteen."

"You have the merchandise?"

"You have an envelope for me?"

Klauswitz used two fingers to withdraw a plain white envelope from beneath his jacket.

"One second."

The Turk faded into the darkness and returned in seconds. He crouched by the mound of a grave and set a leather case between them.

"Hold the light," Klauswitz said, passing it to the other man.

The case was about two feet by one foot and approximately five inches deep. He popped the two clasps and opened the lid, turning the case at the same time so that the light would reveal its contents.

"It is a French F1, Tireur d'Elite, 7.62mm. They say it will consistently group ten rounds into a circle smaller than inches at better than two hundred meters."

The black helmet nodded, and beneath the dark visor Klauswitz's thick lips curled in a smile. "It will."

Dieter Klauswitz had used the French sniper rifle before, but never with a silencer. This one was a beauty, broken down into five parts. The bipod was attached, and the barrel was equipped with a flash hider.

The man behind the visor loved guns. He deeply regretted that he would have to abandon this one after it had done its work.

"How clean is it?"

"Stolen in Marseilles two weeks ago," the Turk replied. "Absolutely untraceable. Do you need ammo?"

"No. That's been taken care of." Klauswitz passed the envelope over and closed the lid of the case.

"Good hunting," the Turk chuckled, and the two men faded into the darkness in different directions.

Seconds later the steady bass throb of the BMW's engine filled the park, and the rider headed north toward Wedding and Wiebe Strasse.

Gertrude Klammer backed the Mercedes into the dirt-floored garage. She killed the lights and the engine, and left all the keys on the front seat.

The envelope was beneath the bricks just as the message said. Gertrude didn't bother to check the contents. She knew the thousand marks would be there.

Stuffing it into her purse, she stepped out onto the walk of Wiebe Strasse and carefully closed the door. When the padlock was snapped, she hurried toward the lights of the larger Moabit Allee.

The Wedding section frightened her. It was full of empty houses too run-down for the landlords to repair. Young, hippie-type squatters and single foreign workers occupied them because they could do so for nothing.

But there were also criminals of all kinds in the area. She was elated to find a cruising cab within two blocks.

Unknown to Fräulein Gertrude Klammer, she had a protector. He sat on the BMW at the other end of Wiebe Strasse in the darkness between two houses. He didn't move until the woman was safely in the cab and it was speeding away.

The last thing Klauswitz wanted was for this woman to be molested in any way. It would be a disaster for the police to question her reasons for being in the Wedding section alone at this hour.

He didn't start the bike. He pushed it to Number 9 and unlocked the door with the second key Hessling had provided.

Inside, he was the epitome of efficiency. He closed the door tightly and snapped the BMW's light on, aiming it so the beam illuminated the rear of the garage and the Mercedes. Then, from the rafters of the garage, he took down a wicker picnic basket and a suitcase.

The wicker basket contained sandwiches, fruit, and a thermos of juice. He lifted everything out and put the gun case in the bottom of the basket. When the thermos and food were replaced, the basket was filled perfectly to the lid.

The suitcase went into the trunk of the car. Inside it was a briefcase and the complete wardrobe of a traveling businessman.

Quickly, Klauswitz stripped out of the leather and boots.

Beneath them he was completely naked. From the suitcase he donned socks, shorts, dark blue pinstripe trousers, and a white-on-white shirt. He carefully knotted a light blue tie and slipped into the suit jacket.

Everything fit, including a pair of black Gucci loafers, imprinted on the inside heel with the mark of the Italian shoemaker's Fifth Avenue store in New York City.

In fact, all the clothes bore American labels.

He removed the jacket and shoes, and placed them on the Mercedes's rear seat. Carefully, retaining the knot in the tie, he removed it and placed it on the jacket.

It was a bit of a struggle to get the leathers on over the clothing, but he managed.

Next he checked the briefcase.

The papers were all in order and scrupulously accurate. They detailed recent business transactions between Mockdendorf Limited of West Berlin, a toy manufacturer, and Klein Enterprises of Albany, New York.

Mockdendorf was a very real company, with offices in West Berlin, Hamburg, and Frankfurt.

Klein Enterprises was a fiction, but the Vopo guards at Checkpoint Charlie would never know that.

He replaced the papers and picked up a passport packet. Inside, he found a U.S. passport issued in the name of David Klein. Address: 414-C Shamrock Towers, Albany, New York. Occupation: President, Klein Enterprises.

He flipped to the back pages of the passport where frontier stamps were placed. David Klein had entered the West German Republic two days before, via Frankfurt.

The passport photograph was of a blond-haired, smiling Dieter Klauswitz.

Also in the packet was a payment voucher for the Metropol Hotel. This he would need in order to stay overnight in the German Democratic Republic. And he had to stay overnight, because the remaining item in the packet was a first-class ticket on Tuesday morning's Aeroflot flight from East Berlin to London's Heathrow Airport.

*Well done*, Dieter thought, *very well done. I commend you, Herr Oskar Hessling.*

The last item in the briefcase was a small, square box. Inside it were ten 7.62mm steel-cased shells. Each one of them had been doctored, a minuscule amount of potassium cyanide inserted in their tips.

Klauswitz was sure he would need only one, two at the most, but he emptied all ten of the shells into the zippered pocket of his black leather jacket.

He closed and locked the doors and the trunk lid of the sedan, and then surveyed the car and the garage.

Everything was in readiness for his return the following day.

After securely attaching the wicker basket to the rear of the bike, he wheeled it from the garage and locked the door. On Moabit Allee he cranked the big machine and roared south toward the brighter lights of downtown Berlin.

As he rode, he retraced the plan and the escape route. He had gone over it three times in minute detail in his mind by the time he parked the machine at the foot of the Insulaner Mountain.

At the end of the war, Berlin was rubble. Before the rebuilding process could start, huge amounts of twisted steel, concrete, bricks, and other debris had to be disposed of or burned.

The solution that was eventually adopted was to heap the scattered rubble into huge artificial hills, cover them with soil in a tiered effect, and plant the whole with grass, shrubs, and small trees. As a result, these rubble ''mountains'' now dotted the skyline of Berlin.

The largest of them was the Insulaner, soaring 260 feet into the air. From its peak most of West Berlin could be seen.

But come the next morning, Dieter Klauswitz would be interested in only one piece of West Berlin real estate: the wide, sweeping steps of the American Memorial Library. It was on those steps, in a little more than twelve hours, that several West German dignitaries and the American, Stephan Conway, would speak.

Klauswitz removed the wicker basket from the rear of the BMW and strolled across Mehring Damm to a phone booth.

He deposited the correct coins and dialed. The phone was answered on the first ring. He easily recognized the now-familiar wheeze.

"Herr Hessling, this is Pilgrim."

"*Ja, mein Herr*. The car?"

"Fine, and the suitcases as well."

"Excellent," came the wheeze. "And the papers?"

"Also fine. Everything is go."

"I have already informed our employer. The money should reach me within the hour. It will be deposited in the Bahamas account ten seconds after the newscast confirming."

"It has been a pleasure doing business with you."

"*Danke. Auf Wiedersehen, Herr Pilgrim.*"

"*Auf Wiedersehen, Herr Hessler.*"

Dieter Klauswitz walked back across the boulevard, around the fence that bordered the swimming pool that had been built on the lower tier of the rubble mountain, and began climbing the Insulaner.

Oskar Hessling poked the telephone's disconnect button and strained his stubby fingers toward the half-eaten box of chocolates. He popped one into his mouth, chewed, and washed it down with a slurping drink of schnapps.

"Good man," he wheezed, and burped, "damned good man. I knew he would be. And a loner. Perfect."

Oskar Hessling had a habit of talking out loud to himself. Often he would ask himself questions and give himself answers. It had come from years of being alone. It was only one of the myriad oddities about the man. Another was the fact that, in the vast twenty-odd rooms of the mansion where he now sat, there was not a single mirror.

The reason for this was because Oskar Hessling could not stand to look at himself.

He was huge. Not even corpulent, grossly fat, or obese could describe the 450 pounds of flab and blubber that rolled in waves beneath his tentlike clothing.

His jowls hung far below his chin on either side, and his

eyes were like tiny dark holes in the sickly white balloon of
his face.

But as fat and grossly ugly as Oskar Hessling was, it did
not affect the cunning of his razor-sharp mind. Unlike
Hans-Otto Voigt—the other master of crime in West
Berlin—Hessling needed no army of stooges around him. He
did everything necessary to amass his great wealth with just
his bank of telephones.

Now he squinted in deep concentration. In two seconds he
came up with the number he desired from over five hundred
in the memory bank of his phenomenal mind.

"*Ja?*"

"*Guten Morgen, Fräulein.* The pilgrim has landed."

"I understand."

"I can expect you soon?"

"Mein Herr, I think it would be wiser—"

"My dear lady, I have survived these many years by being
extremely careful. I shall expect you in fifteen minutes."

"But . . ."

The dial tone filled the room from the phone's speaker
box. Hessling punched up a new number. He didn't have to
think to dial this one. He used it often.

"The Golden Calf."

"Put Antonio on!"

"Certainly, Herr Hessling."

The Golden Calf was just one of the many slightly sleazy
nightclubs Hessling owned on or around the Ku'Damm
featuring female strippers or male transvestites.

"*Ja, mein Herr?*"

"*Guten Morgen.* Are you busy, Tony?"

"Only fair."

"Good, good. I have a tender morsel arriving soon, Tony.
Class and looks, a real beauty. You will enjoy her."

"The usual fee, mein Herr?"

"Of course, my boy . . . and perhaps a little bonus. This
is very special. Shall we say an hour?"

"I'll be there."

"Good."

He broke the connection, thought, and dialed yet again. The London number rang several times before the brusque tones of a female voice on an answering machine came through.

"Peter Limpton's office. Mr. Limpton is not in. If you will leave your name, number, and message at the tone, Mr. Limpton will return your call as soon as possible."

Hessling waited until the dull tone sounded, then wheezed out his message. "I believe I will be able to deliver the shipment of radio parts after all, Mr. Limpton. If you will please call me in a day or so at the Berlin number I gave you, we can discuss the financial arrangements."

As the dial tone filled the room, Hessling managed a laugh. It hurt his chest. He washed another chocolate down with schnapps, and dialed the last number he would need that night.

"Stasis, Corporal Kleimann."

"Colonel Balenkov, *bitte*."

"*Bitte*."

Stasis was short for *Staatssicherheitsdienst*, the East German state security service. Colonel Volatory Balkenkov was Moscow's KGB liaison to Stasis.

Hessling wiped drool from his chin and smiled as he waited. He delighted in his own cleverness. He would soon have it all, and what better way to force the American to sell him the goods than to enlist the aid of the Russians. They needn't know that he was selling the goods right back to them through Peter Limpton.

"Balenkov."

"*Guten Morgen, mein Herr*," Hessling rasped.

"Ah, Hessling. I was wondering when you were going to call. What do I get for my little favors?"

"As yet, Colonel, I am not sure. But the prospect for reward is great. Sometime in the late afternoon, today, an American, David Klein, will check into the Metropol."

"Yes?"

"His real name is Dieter Klauswitz. He's a West German, currently out on parole and awaiting trial for robbery. That should be enough to hold him for a few days, shouldn't it?"

"More than enough. But why?"

"I must make a contact or two on Tuesday. I'll call you that evening and let you know what to do with him, and how great both our rewards will be. *Auf Wiedersehen*, Colonel."

"*Wiedersehen*, Herr Hessling."

Hessling pushed the disconnect button and poured himself another glass of schnapps. He wouldn't be needing the telephone anymore.

He could almost see the Russian's face grow florid and hear the curses being thrown at him over the wall.

Hessling didn't care. He had provided many services for the Russian pig. This, in the end, would be another one. Needless to say, the service would also swell Hessling bank accounts to bursting.

But enough of business, he thought. It was time to contemplate the pleasures that would take place shortly.

Antonio and the woman.

His heart was already palpitating too much. He would have to be careful and not get too excited.


She parked several blocks away and walked down the winding street lined by tall hedges. Over them she could see the slate roofs and soaring gables of huge, stately houses against the dark sky.

It was easy to spot Herr Oskar Hessling's mansion. It was larger and grander than all the others on the street.

With a slightly shaking hand, she pushed the button on the entry buzzer. She disliked doing business in the wee hours of the morning.

"*Ja?*" said a voice through the speaker grille.

"I am at the gate."

"Ah, yes, Fräulein, come in. The front door is unlocked."

There was a buzz and the gate popped open. She stepped through and closed it behind her.

The house sat well back from the street at the round of a U-shaped, tree-lined drive. It was deathly quiet other than the tapping of her heels on the cobbled walk. The front door opened with a grating sound from the hinges, and she stepped into a long, high-ceilinged hall with huge oak doors leading into well-appointed rooms on either side.

"The last door on the right, my dear. It is my study."

The voice came from a small speaker secreted somewhere in the wall above her.

The house was baronial, with dark, wood-paneled walls, rough-hewn ceiling beams, ornately carved balconies, displays of stuffed animals, and brooding tapestries. There were even crossed sabers and a knight's helmet over the fireplace at the end of the hall.

Hessling sat in the special chair that had been designed and reinforced to accommodate his huge bulk. Ranged on the horseshoe desk around him were television screens, computer consoles, and the telephones he used to run his empire.

The room was as gargantuan as its owner, and the walls, floor to ceiling, were lined with leather-bound tomes. She was sure that not a single one of them had ever been opened.

"*Guten Morgen, Fräulein.*"

"Herr Hessling."

"You are even more beautiful than at our last meeting."

Hessling could feel the pressure in his pounding heart as he watched her glide across the room. Her amazing body was draped in an expensive black dress that stylishly revealed richly curved hips, flaring thighs, and jutting breasts.

The woman wasn't a classic beauty, but she was vibrant and eroticism seemed to ooze from her. And even more than her sensuality, Hessling sensed that beneath that calm, cold beauty lay a full-blown predator.

Hessling liked that. It added spice to what he was going to force her to do.

Dismissing the leer in his piglike eyes—and trying not to look at his grossness with her own—the woman set the briefcase on the desk beside him. She flipped the catches and opened the lid. "It's all there . . . in dollars."

Before she could retreat, he grabbed her arm. Her stomach churned as his thick lips slobbered over the back of her hand.

"You're shaking, my dear."

"Why shouldn't I?" she murmured. "It isn't often I arrange to have someone murdered."

"True. But I think you also shake because you find me repugnant."

This time she met his gaze directly. "Yes, I do," she replied, snatching her arm from his grasp and stepping back.

His massive shoulders shrugged. "No matter. It doesn't bother me. Everyone, my entire life, has found me repugnant. I've learned to feed on it."

"Would you please count the money? I have to get back. Needless to say, I have a long day ahead of me."

"Yes, you do, don't you." He laughed, and it instantly turned into a gasping wheeze. It was several moments before he got his breathing back under control. "The bar is there, against the wall. Fix yourself a drink."

She didn't want to spend a minute more than necessary with him, but a drink would help. She could feel his tiny eyes peeling away her clothing as she poured liquor into a glass.

When she turned back to face him, it was even worse. As his meaty hands extracted the bound bundles of one-hundred-dollar bills from the briefcase, his eyes never left her.

She shivered. She felt as though he were actually raping her with his eyes.

"I have done some checking . . . made a few inquiries."

"So?"

"I know who you are, Fräulein. I know your connections, and from a few deductions I think I can safely say that you are not doing this entirely on your own initiative."

"You have been paid," she said, trying in vain to keep a nervous quiver out of her voice. "Whatever you know, the money is to buy your silence as well as the deal."

"I think not." He finished stacking the money and gave her his full attention. "I think my silence requires an added payment of sorts."

"How much?"

"Oh, not monetary."

"What, then?" The eyes narrowed until she could hardly see the pupils at all. Her whole body was shaking now.

"You are very beautiful, Fräulein. Your body beneath that

clothing is, I'm sure, a work of art. I would like to see you naked."

"You're mad."

"No, not mad . . . lustful. Under this bulk I am a volcano of seething lust."

"You mean you want me to . . ."

"Have sex? Yes. But not with me. I cannot, you see. My doctors tell me the excitement would kill me. My heart, you know."

She set the glass down on the bar. Her hands were trembling so hard now that she couldn't hold it.

"What, then . . ." she stammered.

"I want to *watch* you make love. I have already arranged for a young man to drop by shortly."

"No!"

"He is Italian, and quite handsome. He is also, I assure you, very clean. I do believe, my dear, that in the end you will enjoy it."

"You are mad, completely mad!" she cried, lurching toward him without fully realizing what she was doing. "I won't do it! You can't make me! You daren't say a word! You are as implicated as I!"

"Ah, that is where you are wrong. It would be your word against mine. And I assure you, my dear, I can provide the authorities with enough information that they would look no further than you or your lover."

Suddenly his left hand shot forward and captured her wrist. His strength was immense, and the speed with which he pulled her toward him astounded her.

His right hand was equally as quick and adept as he gathered the front of her dress in his fingers.

"Stop! Stop it, you pig!"

His hand yanked, and the buttons from the bodice to the hem parted. In almost the same movement, his fingers slid beneath one cup of her bra and began to painfully knead her breast.

"Beautiful, sheer perfection," he wheezed.

"Bastard!" she shrieked, and raked the right side of his face with the claws of her left hand.

Blood spouted from four even red lines in his fat cheek. It gathered on his chin and dripped down to spread a crimson stain on his shirt.

But he didn't howl in pain, nor did he remove his hand from her breast. Instead, he smiled.

"A predator . . . a sleek cat with claws. Remove your underwear . . . and we'll have you ready for Tony when he arrives."

His breath was coming in gasps now, so strained that he could hardly utter the words. He was perspiring heavily, and his chest was heaving with obvious effort.

"Your . . . flesh . . . excites . . . me . . ."

Suddenly she stopped trying to get away from him. The rage faded from her face, replaced by a smile. Her eyes narrowed as the idea took hold, and her body became pliant under his hands.

"My body . . . it pleases you?" she purred.

"Shouldn't do this . . . dangerous . . . for me."

"Let go of my arm so I can take off my bra."

"Yes . . . beautiful . . ."

Leaning forward so her scent filled his nostrils, she lifted her legs and slipped off her pumps. Clasping both hands behind her neck, she stretched languidly, like a cat, breasts thrusting upward.

Hessling clasped his own hands to his chest, as if by doing so he could ease the incredible pain he could feel building inside it. He tried to look away, but he found it impossible. Her eyes and her body challenged him to ignore her, to be unaware of what she was offering.

She shrugged and the ripped dress slid over her shoulders, arms, and hips, falling in a heap at her feet. Her figure was exquisite, a voluptuous jewel of perfect proportions. She leaned down to retrieve the dress, full breasts moving impatiently in the tight confines of her bra.

She smiled, placing the dress over a chair. Touching her lower lip with her tongue, she concentrated on rolling the black sheen of panty hose to her ankles, then stepped free. The stomach was flat, the legs firm and delicately muscled, the lines of her body free from bloat or softness.

He gasped in admiration, as much for the practiced performance as for the undeniable beauty.

The lacy bra was so tight it cut into the smooth flesh. Unhooking it, she pulled it down over her arms. Her breasts were high, conical, and tipped with delicate pink.

With a smooth action of her hips, she removed the black panties, tossing them away.

"That's . . . enough, for now," he choked, thumping his chest with his meaty fists. "We shall wait for the boy . . ."

"What for?" she chided, running her hands under and over her breasts.

She stepped forward and took one of his hands. It was balled into a tight fist.

Holding his wrist with one hand, she raked the nails of the other hand down to the curled fingers. When they opened, she thrust the hand between her legs and clamped her thighs over it.

"Oh, God . . . oh, God . . ."

She pulled his head between her breasts and squeezed their soft fullness with her elbows.

Involuntarily, his hand began to move between her legs. Her perfume made his mind reel, and even as he felt breath leaving him, he blubbered between the twin mounds of soft flesh that denied him air.

"Ox . . . oxygen . . ." he gasped, his free hand snaking across the desk.

She saw the movement and stopped it with her own hand.

She speeded up her gyrations. A moaning sound joined his labored breathing. His body was heaving now, and he began to whine. And then the whine turned into a rattle.

Suddenly he lurched, sending her against the desk. He swayed to his feet, clutching his chest, and then toppled with a dull thud to the floor.

"Pig," she hissed, tears streaming from her eyes. "Dirty pig!"

She didn't want to touch him again, but she had to. She practically had to grind her fingers into the folds of flesh at his neck before she was sure he was dead.

She dressed quickly. She found the buttons that had been

pulled from her dress and dropped them into her purse. With paper clips, she fastened the dress, and then returned the stacks of bills to the briefcase.

Then, briefcase and purse in hand, she stood at the door and surveyed the room a last time.

The glass. It was all she had touched besides the front doorknob.

She cleaned the glass with her skirt and used the garment again on the knob as she let herself out.

Barely taking a breath, she ran all the way to her car and tumbled inside.

Then she fell apart.

It was twenty minutes before she could make her fingers work to put the key in the ignition.

As she drove past Hessling's in the predawn darkness, she saw a tall, handsome young man pushing the button.

# FIVE

There was nearly an hour and a half between flights. Carter guessed that Lisa's layover would be about the same.

His first guess as to where she would spend the time was right on the button: the cocktail lounge in the Pan Am concourse of Frankfurt-am-Main Airport.

The way she had sounded on the phone the previous evening, Carter guessed she could use several Bloody Marys.

When he entered the lounge he recognized her immediately even behind the dark glasses and the new, shorter hair style. She was wearing an ice-blue dress that accented high breasts, a slender waist, and softly rounded hips.

Somehow she sensed his approach and spun to face him on the armed stool. Her eyes were even with his, and he wondered what they were doing behind those dark shades.

She didn't smile. Carter hadn't expected she would. He wondered if she were remembering—as he was—that night: the ambush in the hotel room, the chaos of gunfire, the smell of cordite, and the wild ride to the hospital that they had barely reached in time.

"Hello, Lisa."

"Hi. Want to compare scars?"

Now she smiled and the ice broke. He planted his lips gently but firmly on hers, and slid up onto the adjacent stool.

"Thank you for coming."

"I'm on vacation," he shrugged, and nodded to the bartender. "One of those, not too hot."

"This may be just Delaine, you realize. We may be sisters, but we're quite different. She has a tendency to get a little frantic."

Carter sipped the Bloody Mary and smiled. "I'll do what I can, but I really came to see you."

"Let's hope Berlin is just fun."

"Yeah, let's hope."

His antennae were vibrating. It was the sixth sense that every good agent acquired over the years, if he stayed alive.

As Lisa continued to speak, Carter listened with one ear and let his eyes travel around the small lounge; an old woman with a young blond-haired boy; a couple of coed types with hair so long they were sitting on it; a short, gray-haired man reading the morning paper; an older couple in the midst of a quiet argument.

Carter moved his gaze back to the gray-haired man. The eyes behind half glasses came up from behind the pages to meet Carter's.

They stared at each other for a few seconds, and then the man folded his paper. He checked his tab, placed a bill on the table, and left.

The bill was carefully folded and refolded until it resembled a star.

"Lisa . . ."

"Yes?"

"Excuse me for a second, will you? Nature calls."

"Of course."

A waitress was trying to unfold the bill without tearing it as Carter passed. He heard her grumble something about big tip or no big tip, she wished customers wouldn't try to be so cute.

The man was washing his hands as Carter pushed through the door. He saw legs under one of the stall doors, and moved to the door two down.

Their eyes met in the mirror, and both heads barely nodded.

It took almost five minutes before the man emerged from the stall, washed his hands, and left.

"How was your flight from Paris?"

"Fine."

"You are on Pan Am Nine-two-two, I believe."

"Yes, to Berlin."

"Very convenient. Peter Limpton received a call very early this morning in London from one of his West German contacts."

"A buyer or seller?" Carter asked.

"It would appear a seller." He pulled a thin manila envelope from his inside jacket pocket and set it on the mirror tray in front of Carter. "His name is Oskar Hessling. All we have on him is in there."

"What did Limpton have to say?"

"Hessling was putting the squeeze on a big American electronics manufacturer. He had told Limpton earlier that the goods would be pure gold. In fact, worth more than gold to Limpton's people. Evidently, the squeeze didn't work. Hessling called him a couple of weeks ago and said that the deal was off."

"And last night it was back on?"

The man nodded and began to dry his hands. "He directed Limpton to give him a call Tuesday in Berlin. Alma wants you to do a little digging before then."

"Will do."

"Have a nice flight."

Carter returned to the lounge and answered Lisa's quizzical stare with the truth. "Business."

"So you're not on vacation."

"It would seem that I'm not," he replied. "But it's just routine. I'll still look into your problem."

Flight 922 was called for boarding. When they had passed through security, Lisa folded her arm through Carter's and leaned close to his ear.

"Do you travel without your friends now?"

"Oh, no. False bottom in the suitcase I checked."

The "friends" she was referring to were Carter's 9mm Luger, which he affectionately called Wilhelmina, a deadly little stiletto named Hugo, and a walnut-sized gas bomb dubbed Pierre.

Carter actually thought, that sunny morning walking down

the airport concourse with the beautiful and appealing woman on his arm, that he wouldn't need his "friends" on this trip to Berlin.

Every day at noon, the Freiheitsglocke in the American Memorial Library building boomed out the hour. It sounded each noon to remind Berlin and the world that all men derive the right to freedom equally from God.

Dieter Klauswitz cared nothing about symbols or God. About his freedom, he had an undying passion to keep it. He removed the five pieces of his means to keep his freedom from the leather case and began assembling them.

From his sunny, 260-foot-tall perch above Berlin, he had a commanding view of the boulevard in front of the library. On the steps, workmen were putting the finishing touches to the podium and seats with bunting for the rally.

On the sidewalks and in one lane of the partially blocked-off boulevard, the curious, the demonstrators, and the enthusiasts had already begun to gather.

Berlin police manned the barricades, their spotless uniforms and white helmets gleaming. Uniformed and plainclothes SSD, men and officers of the special security department, stood about grim-faced in the heat.

They looked uncomfortable.

Klauswitz himself was slightly uncomfortable. His muscles ached from lying on the ground all night. But not enough to jeopardize his performance. With the added clothing beneath the leather, he was perspiring, but not enough to impair his determination.

When the F1 was completely assembled and checked, he scooted around on his belly until he found the perfect piece of hard, flat ground for the bipod. When this was done, he fit the stock to his shoulder and his eye to the scope.

The line from the open end of the scope down the twenty-eight-inch barrel, over the front sight and the silencer, was clean and pure all the way to the library steps.

An electrician in blue coveralls stood at the podium, connecting and adjusting a bank of microphones.

Klauswitz moved the cross hairs of the scope against the

sight until a button on the man's left breast pocket was sighted in. He adjusted the range, then rolled the magnifier to full.

The button seemed to explode in size in the scope.

"Bang," Klauswitz said, "you're dead."

He popped the box magazine and, one by one, loaded it with the cyanide-treated shells. When the magazine was reset, he made one more sighting calculation.

Perfect.

He scooted over to the wicker basket, withdrew the thermos and sandwiches, and like so many of the workmen below him, proceeded to have his lunch.

The honeyed shade of her dark blond hair, the slant of her eyebrows, and the intense blue eyes were the only physical evidence to the fact that Delaine Berrington Conway was Lisa's sister.

Where Lisa's figure was full and roundly feminine, Delaine's was angular, with small breasts and almost boyishly slim hips.

Even her face, with its sharp bones and planes, lacked the soft character of Lisa's.

At this moment she was dressed in a plain white bra and white panties. She sat at her vanity, idly rolling an eyeliner pencil back and forth between her fingers.

"Jesus Christ, aren't you dressed yet? We have to leave in ten minutes!"

Delaine looked up to see her distinguished-looking husband, her champion of industry, scowling at her from the doorway.

"I really don't feel like going, Stephan."

"Bullshit. You're going, and that's all there is to it!"

Delaine stared at him in the mirror. It wasn't hard to see why she had fallen in love with this man, married him, and endured him for the last four years.

"You have to go, Delaine," he said, his face darkening with menace.

It was a chiseled, leathery face, but not a coarse one. The long nose had been accidentally broken once, but it retained an aquiline grace. And the long, horizontal dimple in his left cheek never lost its appeal, even when he clenched his jaw tightly, as he was doing now. His eyes, normally a warm and moody gray, were now hidden beneath his heavily frowning brow.

"Who was she, Stephan?"

"What?"

"Last night's conquest. Do you have a mistress on your staff over here, or did you bring her with us in the entourage from the States?"

"I don't know what you're talking about."

"It's not like you to pick up a cheap tart off the streets, Stephan. Besides, the perfume I smelled on you last night when you got into bed was too expensive for a tart."

"Delaine, please, do we have to go into this . . ."

"I guess I would rather have it be a tart, though. That means you would forget her the next morning. But you haven't been forgetting this one. And that perfume has become familiar. You should stick to women who use my brand of perfume, Stephan."

"Christ, Delaine, we'll talk about this tonight . . ."

"I want to talk about it now!"

"Well, I don't!" he shouted, and stomped to the closet. With an angry growl, he threw the doors open and bunched the clothing in his big arms.

Then, hangers and all, he walked them to her and dropped them on the floor. He lifted her like a feather from the vanity stool and set her on her feet in the middle of the clothing.

He fumbled in the randomly thrown pile of clothing until he withdrew a dress.

"Put this on and pull yourself together. We'll deal with your paranoia later."

Delaine grimaced in distaste at the garish red dress he thrust into her hands.

"Must I?"

"You must."

"And if I don't?"

"If you don't, little girl, I'll really give you something to divorce me over! I need you on that stand today. It would be a slap in the face of the others if you weren't there, standing by my side.''

"Would you hit me again, Stephan? You're very good at doing that so it doesn't show.''

Without warning, he slammed his balled fist into her stomach. She gasped and crumpled into a fetal ball in the middle of the pile of clothing.

"That answer your question?'' he hissed.

She gagged.

"Ten minutes. Be ready.''

He stomped from the bedroom, and Delaine pulled herself to her feet. Still fighting nausea from the pain, she reached for the red dress. She hated it; it wasn't her style at all, a red, scoop-necked, sheath-skirted design that she considered too bright and cheap-looking for her taste. But Stephan had been adamant when he bought it for the trip.

Until now she had refused to wear it.

"Oh, God,'' she whispered, sliding the slinky garment over her head. "Hurry, Lisa, hurry! Come and take me away from this madman!''


Horst Vintner was a big man with a thick, round neck. The connection was so strong that head, shoulders, and body turned all at the same time, as if one section were immobile without the aid of the other two. The eyes, deep-set and slow-moving, digested all they saw, passing over nothing.

At that moment they were scrupulously scanning the windows and rooftops around the perimeter his men had set up for the rally. Not that he was overly worried. The dignitaries were minor, not really of any interest to what survived of the terrorist groups in West Berlin.

The assignment was actually very routine. Vintner and his SSD team were there to snap pictures and get names, if possible, of the demonstrators. There was no expectation of trouble.

Horst Vintner had been a policeman his entire life. He had chased thieves, con men, rapists, murderers, and terrorists. The job of heading an SSD team to guard visiting VIPs and to control possible demonstrations was merely something to keep him busy until retirement.

Vintner was sixty-two years old, and his retirement was six
months away.

"They are arriving, sir."

"I see that, Bruchner. Pick out two men who look the most
conspicuous and put them on each end of the steps."

"Yes, sir."

"And inform the uniformed officers to block off the rest of
this side of the boulevard."

"Yes, sir."

Vintner's aide moved away through the gathering crowd,
and he applied a match to the bowl of his pipe.

His superiors had told him that morning that there had been
death threats to the American, Stephan Conway. Vintner had
talked to Conway at his hotel shortly after that over the
phone.

"It's probably a sort of personal vendetta more than anything else, Herr Vintner. I was the victim of an attempted
blackmail quite some time ago in the States. I thought that
when I had told them to go to hell, it would die away. But
lately the threats have become more strange."

Vintner didn't inquire into the blackmail. At that point it
wasn't part of his job. Keeping Herr Stephan Conway alive
while he was on German soil *was* his job.

As Horst Vintner puffed his pipe and scanned the crowd,
he wished he were back chasing murderers or retired, one or
the other.

This in-between duty was hell.

As Dieter Klauswitz saw the first speaker step to the
podium he went over the schedule of the rally that Hessling
had given him.

There were to be four speakers in all. The American,
Stephan Conway, would be the last. At the end of his speech,
Conway's wife, and the three German speakers and their
wives, would move to the front of the steps.

There they would stand at attention in a line, while the
anthems of both countries would be played.

"That, Pilgrim, is when you fire. Not before."

He took another range-sighting through the F1 scope, from the man at the podium back down the line of the seated scheduled speakers. He found the erect figure of Stephan Conway dressed in a light tan summer suit. Beside him, in a vivid red dress, her eyes on her lap, was the American businessman's wife.

Oskar Hessling was never a cheap thief. He had started out his life of crime as a procurer of flesh for the brothels of Beirut and the rest of the Middle East. Young virgins from a poverty-stricken Germany were sent into white slavery in these brothels, and if they were especially attractive—blond and buxom—they were shoved on into the harems of desert sheiks.

It was a profitable business, and allowed Hessling to expand. In the years between 1960 and now, he had formed a criminal empire based on dope, prostitution, extortion, blackmail, pornography, and the sale of illegal arms.

It was known that he would buy and/or sell anything to or from the Eastern bloc of nations, including Mother Russia.

It wasn't surprising that Boris Simonov, as Peter Limpton, had set up a channel to do business with Hessling.

What was surprising was the fact that West German authorities knew much of Hessling's business, and yet had never been able to turn a single arrest into an indictment.

Carter, as he slipped the man's file into his briefcase, wondered what he could come up with if the entire security apparatus and police departments of the West German government had been unable to come up with anything.

"You don't sound happy," Lisa said from beside him. "You rarely sigh."

"Dead end," Carter replied, squeezing her hand. "I'll tell you about it later."

They were descending on their final approach to Tegel Airport. From the air, West Berlin looked like a solo piece of a jigsaw puzzle. It was bounded by one hundred miles of concrete wall and the fifty-yard-wide German Democratic Republic "death strip." The sand floor of the "death strip" was meticulously raked fine each morning. Even the mark of a crawling snake could be detected between the two concrete walls.

Carter narrowed his eyes and looked at the city without seeing the wall and the strip. It was huge and beautiful, with its fifty square miles of lakes, parks, and woodlands with deer and wild boar and forests. It was the largest green area of any city in the world and, Carter knew, one of the reasons West Berliners didn't go stir crazy in their isolation from the rest of West Germany.

The landing was smooth, and they were through customs in less than fifteen minutes.

Carter had called ahead to reserve two suites at the Victoria on the Kurfürsten Damm. It was a thirty-minute ride by taxi from Tegel into the center of the city, and they both were silent for most of the trip.

At the door of Lisa's suite, Carter brushed her cheek with his lips.

"You've been up all night. Get a quick nap before seeing your sister at three. I'll make a few phone calls and do some nosing around."

She nodded, gratitude in her eyes, and followed her porter into the suite. Carter moved to his own room down the hall and tipped the porter.

When the man was gone, he sat on the bed by the phone and lit a cigarette. From a narrow break between the leather walls of his wallet, he extracted a thin sheet of foolscap. On it, in Carter's own personal code, were fifty names and telephone numbers.

"*Guten Tag*, World Bank."

"Jamil Erhanee, *bitte*."

"*Bitte*."

He had to go through two more secretaries before he heard the familiar voice speaking German with a heavy Indian accent.

"Jamil, this is Nick Carter. How's it going?"

"Oh, Christ, the Russians are coming over the wall at last. How long do we have?"

Carter chuckled. "Not quite as bad as all that, my friend. In fact, I'm here more for social reasons than business."

"That's so much crap, but it is good to hear you're still alive."

"Thanks so much. I'd like to pick your brains, memories of your sordid youth."

"Where are you?"

"The Victoria, on the Ku'Damm."

"I'm in the middle of it until around six."

"That's all right. How about seven in the hotel bar?"

"Sounds good. Anything—or anyone—you're particularly interested in?"

"Yeah, a top dog named Oskar Hessling."

"Oh, my, let's make it the Golden Calf then. It's a transvestite club on Roscher Strasse, off the Ku'Damm."

"Suits me. Any particular reason?"

"Yeah. Hessling owns it. He drops in now and then. Who knows, you may see the fat pig in person."

"Seven it is. *Ciao*."

"*Wiedersehen*."

Carter punched out his cigarette and lay back on the bed. If anyone could tell him about or get him close to Oskar Hessling, it was Jamil Erhanee.

It was quite a few hours until seven, and nothing would be happening between now and then besides Lisa's meeting with her sister at three.

Carter closed his eyes. He could use a nap himself.

# SIX

Dieter Klauswitz's hands beneath the black driving gloves were sweating slightly. That was understandable, and Klauswitz knew it wasn't fear. It was anticipation, the anticipation of properly executing a well-engineered plan with tremendous rewards at its end.

As Stephan Conway finished his speech, he stepped back from the podium. The sound of equal cheering and jeering from the crowd reached Klauswitz's ears, but he closed it out.

Now all of his attention was riveted to the top steps of the library. The three Germans, their wives on their arms, stood. In a line, vague smiles plastered on their faces, they moved forward toward Conway.

The woman in the red dress sat, immobile, as she had through all the speeches, including her husband's.

"Move, damn you, move!" Klauswitz hissed, seeing the frown on Conway's face.

At last the American stepped back, took his wife by one elbow, and tugged her forward with him. As the strains of the West German anthem filled the air, partially quieting the crowd, the tan suit and the red dress joined the line.

The F1 was a bolt-action rifle. The marksman slid the bolt back and then forward, jamming one of the deadly shells into the chamber. He disengaged the safety behind the trigger, and then caressed the trigger itself with his right index finger.

71

"Damn, damn, damn," he hissed as the anthem went on and on and both of them remained closed off from his line of fire by others in the line.

Now the first thought of fear entered Klauswitz's mind.

What if they stayed like that through the American anthem? He would never get a clear shot. And then there would be milling around before moving down the steps to the limousines.

"Damn!"

"The Star-Spangled Banner" built, and sweat popped out in beads on Klauswitz's forehead.

Then it happened. Conway took a step forward, his back ramrod straight, his big shoulders squared, his knuckles almost white where he gripped his wife's elbow.

She had no choice but to step forward as well.

Klauswitz inhaled, exhaled slowly, until nearly all breath was expelled and his entire body was relaxed.

Then he squeezed.

Horst Vintner was standing thirty feet in front of the podium and slightly to the side at the bottom of the steps. He made his body rigid as it reacted to the martial music.

But his eyes never stopped moving. They swept the steps and the people on them constantly.

It was Vintner who reacted first when he saw the red dress just above the woman's left breast explode.

The hand-held radio was at his lips and he was running up the steps as fast as his sixty-two-year-old legs would carry him.

"Seal off all the streets as far as two over from the Mehring! Stop all traffic from leaving the boulevard as well! The woman has been shot!"

Vintner saw everything at once as he plowed into Stephan Conway's gut.

The woman was already dead, her eyes still open, staring dumbly as she slipped to the steps.

His two men were running toward the center of the steps, and the others stood, staring and flatfooted. None of them had, as yet, realized what was happening.

Vintner and Conway hit the steps in a pile. They had barely stopped rolling when, less than a foot from Conway's shoulder, Vintner saw a long gouge appear in the concrete. He heard the ricochet, and saw a uniformed officer near the library door grab his right thigh.

Vintner covered Conway's body with his own. "Lie still! Don't move!"

"My wife . . ."

"Your wife is dead. He's still shooting!" Vintner rolled to his back, and heard Conway grunt from the weight.

Everything flashed through the veteran policeman's mind and across his eyes at the same instant.

The wide walk at the foot of the steps and the boulevard beyond were chaos. The two ends of the Mehring and the wider perimeter seemed calm other than massed traffic.

Everyone was doing his job.

*Angle was from above . . . the woman wasn't lifted from her feet by the force of the slug . . . she was driven down and back . . . the second slug was also from above . . . nearly straight down into the concrete.*

Vintner's eyes cased the roofs of the office buildings and high-rise apartment houses across the boulevard even as he barked this information into his radio.

"The roofs! Don't let anyone—man, boy, woman, or dog—out of the area!"

The replies came fast and furious.

"All building exits secured, sir!"

"Mehring secured!"

"Perimeter tight, sir!"

Vintner lowered the radio. "Bruchner!"

"Here, sir!"

The man was already crouching at Vintner's shoulder, his own body adding to the shield over Conway, his service revolver in his hand.

"There was a uniform hit, back by the door."

"Yes, sir, in the thigh. But he's dead."

"Good God, did it hit an artery?"

"No, sir, just a scrape on the side of the leg, but he's dead."

Vintner's experienced brain was already putting it together.

Flesh wound, but it killed.

Cyanide-tipped bullets.

A professional hit.


Dieter Klauswitz had barely seen the result of the second slug before the helmet was on his head and he was hurtling down the other side of the Insulaner.

He covered the distance to the swimming pool in seconds, and even though he had sprinted full tilt, he was breathing normally when he slowed to a walk.

He took the steps calmly to the street level, one at a time, and fired up the BMW. The traffic on that side of the Insulaner was not yet even aware of the chaos on the other side in front of the library.

He headed south on Tempelhofer Damm, past the old airport. Around him, going in both directions, were cyclists dressed exactly like himself. At the south end of Steglitz, he bore right.

In a huge arc that would take him nearly three quarters of the way around the city, he rode, using main arteries and side streets about equally.

Avoiding the east-west highway, he zigzagged through all side streets in smaller residential neighborhoods toward Zehlendorf. At the park, he struck north again toward Hallensee. Once there, he zipped onto the highway and ground the throttle open.

At eighty-five miles an hour it took him no time to reach the Muller Strasse cutoff and drop down into Wedding.

Wiebe Strasse was deserted except for one old man at its north end who didn't look up as Klauswitz idled past.

Inside the garage, with the door closed, he checked the time.

With the mobility of the motorcycle over a car, he had traveled practically three quarters of West Berlin's ring in fourteen minutes.

He stripped out of the leathers and threw them aside. The tie went on first, under the collar and knotted, then the jacket.

He transferred the suitcase and briefcase to the front of the car, and two minutes after pulling into the garage on the BMW, he pulled out in the white Mercedes.

He turned north toward Tegel Airport, always moving away from the scene. As it had been with the BMW, there were white Mercedeses around him at almost every stoplight.

At the traffic circle in front of the airport, there was a roadblock.

He had expected it. He could have avoided it by using one of the smaller streets to go around Tegeler Lake, but instead he joined the line. There were only three cars in front of him.

"*Guten Tag, mein Herr.*"

"*Guten Tag.* What's the trouble?"

"Just a check for insurance cards, mein Herr."

Deiter Klauswitz handed over the rental car papers. The officer scarcely glanced at them.

"You are taking the airport road, mein Herr?"

"No, I have business in the Spandau district. I'm an American."

The man's expression changed at once. He scanned the passport briefly and handed it back. "Very good, Herr Klein. You may go out of the line here. The Schwarzer Weg south around the See. It will be faster."

"Thank you."

"*Bitte sehr.*"

He wheeled the Mercedes out of the line and made the left turn that would take him down to the scenic, tree-lined Schwarzer Weg and around the huge lake. He drove well within the speed limit. According to his watch, he still had twenty-three minutes.

Around the lake, he crossed over the Hovel River and speeded up on the Nellendover Strasse north.

At Spandau Prison he made the huge arc that went around the grounds and found the tourist parking lot. He rescued the briefcase and suitcase, locked the car, and walked back to the boulevard after placing the keys on top of the left front tire under the fender well.

It took him thirty seconds to flag down a passing cab.

"Where to, mein Herr?"

"The Ruhleben U-Bahn."

*"Bitte, mein Herr."*

The taxi lurched forward. Dieter Klauswitz leaned back in the seat and lit the first cigarette he had had in twelve hours.

He peeled the thin black driving gloves from his hands and stuffed them into his jacket pocket. He would deposit them in a trash receptacle in the subway station.

So far . . . perfect. With only one step to go.

With the usual German efficiency and concentration on detail, the area had been sealed off within seconds after the shooting. Now pedestrians were being let out one by one, and each was thoroughly searched. All vehicular traffic was still quarantined.

Horst Vintner had set up a command post in the front reading room of the library. Through the tall windows he had a commanding view of the entire area, and more radiophones had been brought in for added communications.

There were roadblocks on all the roads through West Berlin, as well as the four routes through the wall that led to the autobahn and West Germany. All private planes had been grounded at Tempelhof and Tegel airports, and roadblocks had been erected at the access roads to Tegel and the commercial airlines.

"Herr Vintner . . ."

*"Ja?"*

"They have finished with the on-sight and are ready to remove the bodies."

*"Ja."* Vintner nodded, scratching his initials on the form shoved in front of him. In Germany, he thought ruefully, everything but a normal bowel movement required a form and a signature.

"Herr Conway would like to return to his hotel."

The chief inspector nodded and waved his hand.

"Herr Vintner . . ."

*"Ja,* Bruchner?"

"All the roofs have been checked. Nothing. The office-by-office and room-by-room search is also nearly completed, and also nothing."

"He had to get rid of the rifle. Garbage cans, autos, sewers . . .?"

"Checked, mein Herr. Nothing."

"Dammit, Bruchner! It's only a six-block area and we've got three hundred men out there!"

"I know, mein Herr, but . . ."

Vintner put his elbows on the table and his chin in his hands. He slowed everything down: the adrenaline pumping through his veins, his mental processes, and the sweep of his eyes.

"Where . . . where did the bastard fire from?"

He started to his right, at the Mehring Gate. No, the angle was wrong.

Mentally he moved his own body out to the steps. He placed it just as he remembered Delaine Conway's stance, slightly turned to her left, decreasing his own six-foot height to her five-foot-eight.

His eyes traveled along the roofs of the buildings across the Mehring Damm for the hundredth time in the last hour. And for the hundredth time he came up with nothing.

But for the first time he continued on to the left, down Mehring Damm . . . and then up.

"The Insulaner," he whispered.

"What?"

"The Insulaner, Bruchner! The Insulaner! Take four teams, ten men each, and go up the Insulaner. Start at the top on this side and work your way down!"

"*Ja*, Herr Vintner."

That was it. Vintner was sure of it. The Insulaner.

God, it would be well over four hundred meters.

The son of a bitch was one hell of a shot, even if he did miss his primary target.

Dieter Klauswitz's timing was perfect. He arrived trackside precisely two minutes before the 2:41 express U-Bahn to Schlesisches Tor pulled in.

He sat in one of the seats looking forward. He shouldn't have. Watching all the small stops fly by only added tension. But then tension and danger were part of it.

He only counted the express stops: Olympia Stadium . . . Neu-Westend . . . Theodor-Heuss-Platz. . . .

Sweat was soaking the back of his shirt, but he welcomed it. The last few minutes were always the worst. Once you had the loot and you stepped back out the window or onto the roof to make your final escape, that was always the worst part.

Kaiser Damm . . . Sophie-Charlotte-Platz . . . Bismarck Strasse. . . .

It was a cross-city interchange and a long stop. A woman of immense proportions and a florid face oozed into the seat beside him.

"*Guten Tag, mein Herr.*"

"*Gut* . . . good afternoon, madam." He had to remember: English from here on in. He was just a businessman, no knowledge of German other than their wonderful ability to manufacture cheap toys.

Deutsche Oper . . . Ernst-Reuter-Platz . . . Zoologischer Garten. . . .

"*Engländer?*"

"*Nein* . . . no, I'm an American."

"Ach, I am so sorry."

"Sorry?"

"*Ja. Der Amerikaner.* Herr Stephan Conway. He vas shot at der library a little while ago."

Klauswitz wished the fat old lady spoke no English. "That's terrible!"

"*Ja.*"

Wittenberg-platz . . . Nollendorf-platz . . . the Ku'Damm. . . .

Right about now he would be passing almost under his old apartment. Klauswitz willed the train to go faster between stations and the stops to be shorter.

Gleisdreieck . . . Mockernbruke. . . .

"Ladies and gentlemen . . . Hallesches Tor, Hallesches Tor . . ."

Klauswitz gathered his bags and stood. "My stop."

"*Wiedersehen.*"

"Good-bye, madam."

He emerged into the sunlight blinking, and forced down

the urge to look over his shoulder, down the Mehring Damm, and see the result of the chaos he had caused nearly an hour and a half before.

He had shot the woman and traversed nearly the entire city of West Berlin twice by four modes of transportation: motorcycle, auto, taxi, and U-Bahn.

Now he was back, three blocks north from where the deed had been committed, just outside the police security perimeter, and using his fifth and final mode of transportation: his feet.

Swinging his bags jauntily, he walked north along Friedrich Strasse. The American soldiers on the West German side of Checkpoint Charlie barely glanced at the cover of his passport and nodded.

Unlike their *Volkspolizei* counterparts fifty yards away, they could care less who left the city.

"Your papers, mein Herr."

The Vopo corporal's face, beneath his coal-scuttle helmet, was youthful but hard. The icy blue eyes never left Klauswitz's as he passed over his passport and prepaid entry visa.

"You know of the midnight curfew, Herr Klein?"

"Yes, I do, but I am staying the night and flying out of the GDR in the morning."

Klauswitz passed over the Metropol Hotel one-night voucher and the prepaid Aeroflot ticket. He kept his eyes on the AKM 7.62mm assault rifle and the gray five-button tunic behind it as the man examined the remainder of his papers.

"Very good, Herr Klein. You may change your currency at that first window."

"Thank you."

"*Bitte.*"

The Vopo almost had a smile on his face as Klauswitz moved to the window. The East Germans and the Russians were always happy to oblige anyone who wanted to spend lots of dollars or marks on Aeroflot instead of Western commercial airlines.

To enter East Germany, a traveler must change twenty-five West German marks for twenty-five East German marks, and this money must be spent in the GDR. Also, all money of any kind must be declared.

Klauswitz had his twenty-five marks ready by the time he reached the window. Another Vopo, this one with a twelve-year chevron on his arm, took the money and handed Klauswitz a currency declaration voucher.

He filled it out, got his GDR marks, and picked up his bags.

"Customs there, mein Herr."

Klauswitz crossed the aisle and placed his bags on a table.

The customs inspector spoke to him in German.

"I'm sorry, I speak very little German," Klauswitz replied, proud of the fact that he had not rattled an automatic reply.

"Are any of these things dutiable?" the man asked in English.

"No, no, everything is for my personal use. I have business papers in the briefcase."

The check of the suitcase was perfunctory. Each paper in the briefcase was read.

"You do business here?"

"Not this time," Klauswitz replied, smiling. "Perhaps next time."

"*Ja*. Pass."

Klauswitz picked up his bags and walked on up Friedrich Strasse, past the Unter den Linden, and ten minutes later entered the lobby of the Metropol.

Horst Vintner stood staring down at the French F1 sniper rifle. In one hand he held the magazine. In the other hand he held the two spent shell casings and the remaining eight rounds of live ammunition.

"It's a good thing," Bruchner said from his side, "that he didn't have time for a third shot. He would have gotten Conway for sure."

"*Ja*, for sure," Vintner replied, his brows meeting in a frown.

He had already examined the tips of the live shells. He wouldn't have to get the autopsy results on the two bodies to know that they had been doctored with cyanide. He'd seen the method used too often.

In the hands of a good shooter, this ammo, with this rifle, was accurate and deadly at an even longer range than the Insulaner to the library.

The doctored shells and the choice of weapon told Vintner that he was dealing with not just a shooter, but a flat-out expert marksman and a pro.

The woman had caught it right in the heart. The slug killed her probably before the cyanide could even take effect.

Horst Vintner didn't like it. It smelled.

"Herr Chief Inspector . . ."

"*Ja?*"

"We might have something . . . two witnesses."

Carter had set the timer on the television before he dozed off. The announcer's voice awakened him, but it was several seconds before the man's monotonal voice became words in his brain. When it did, he sat bolt upright in the bed and glued his eyes to the screen.

". . . fortunately, there was not time for the assassin to attempt a third shot. Even with that, according to our footage and eyewitness reports, it was only the quick action of SSD Chief Inspector Horst Vintner that saved the life today of American industrialist Stephan Conway."

Carter was already reaching for his jacket as a camera panned up over the heads of the crowd to Stephan and Delaine Conway standing on the steps of the library. Suddenly he saw Delaine Conway crumple against her husband and a tall, stocky man surge from the crowd.

"However, the incident—as you can see—did have tragic consequences. The assassin did claim two victims. Mrs. Conway—the former Virginia socialite Delaine Berrington—died instantly from a bullet wound in the upper chest. The second victim . . ."

Carter didn't hear the rest. He was already out the door and hurtling down the hall. He pounded a fist on first one door of Lisa's suite and then the other.

"Lisa . . . Lisa! Are you in there? Answer me!"

"May I help you, mein Herr?"

A plump-faced maid, a huge ring of keys hanging from a long chain around her neck, stood in the middle of the hall.

"Open the door! Hurry!"

"*Nein, mein Herr.*"

"*Ja! Schnell!* Quickly!" Carter roared.

"*Ja, ja, ja,*" the woman replied, and with obvious reluctance she jangled a key into the lock.

Carter burst into the room. He analyzed the entire scene at a glance.

Lisa had done the same thing he had done, used the timer on the television to wake her up. She had been in the process of dressing when the announcement had come on. Now she sat, white-faced, wide-eyed, catatonic on the side of the bed, staring at the screen.

She wore a skirt and bra, and a blouse was pulled over only one shoulder.

"Lisa . . ." Carter approached her closely. "Lisa . . ."

The head turned, the eyes grew wider, and then she started screaming.

"*Mein Gott!*" the maid cried out, and lurched toward the door.

"Stay here!" Carter bellowed, enveloping Lisa in his powerful arms, locking hers to her sides and her body to his. "Doctor . . . is there a doctor?"

"*Ja!*" The maid had to shout to be heard over Lisa's hysterical screams.

"The phone . . . get him up here!"

It took only a couple of minutes, and the man was all efficiency when he arrived. While Carter held her to the bed, the physician gave her a sedative, straight to her system through a vein in her right arm.

In short, clipped sentences, Carter explained.

"Shock," the doctor said when he had finished. "Perhaps a hospital would be best for a day or two. Are you her husband?"

"Friend, close friend. I agree, a hospital."

By the time two attendants arrived with a gurney, Lisa had calmed. She was nearly out as they strapped her down, but she managed to speak.

"Nick . . ."

"Yes, Lisa?"

"Nick . . . Nick . . ."

"I'm here, Lisa, I'm right here."

He grasped her hand. Her eyes opened, wavered, and eventually found his.

"It's wrong, Nick . . . it's wrong."

"Yeah, baby . . ."

"He did it, Nick . . . Stephan killed her . . ."

"Lisa . . ."

She was fading fast, but just as her eyes closed, he heard her say one more thing: "That dress . . . terrible. Delaine would never wear that dress . . ."

# SEVEN

"I am sorry, Herr Carter, but the chief inspector cannot see you."

She was big, buxom, blonde, and looked as if she should be carrying a spear in a Wagnerian opera. She was also, according to everyone he had seen already, the only path to Horst Vintner, the man who had the answers to all the questions rattling through Carter's brain.

"Look, all I want to do, Fräulein . . ."

"Metzger . . . Maria Magdalena Metzger."

"Well, Fräulein Metzger, if I could just talk to him for a few minutes—"

"*Nein.* He is much too busy now to see an American private detective. *Guten Tag.*"

Before Carter realized it, she had maneuvered him into the hall and slammed the door of her office in his face.

"Dammit," he growled, and nailed the first person he passed, a short brunette with huge glasses and a frown that covered her whole face. "Fräulein . . ."

"*Ja?*"

She didn't stop, and Carter had to walk fast to keep up with her. "Is there a telephone around here?"

"Are you authorized?"

"It doesn't look like it."

"Then there is a public pay phone on the main floor by the side entrance."

She was gone and so was Carter, down the stairs.

He used the hot-line number to West Berlin's AXE offices, but when a female voice answered, he didn't request the scrambler. He just barked.

"This is Carter, N3! Get me Marty Jacobs . . . now!"

She moved. *Click, click, whirr, whirr,* and the head of AXE Berlin was on the line.

"Jesus, Nick, you didn't check in when you arrived. I didn't know you were in town."

"I was going to, later. Marty, I need action, and I need it now."

Quickly, Carter gave the man a rundown on events and what he wanted.

"I don't know, Nick—this guy Vintner's a hard nut, an old hand."

"I don't give a damn if he's Adolf reincarnate, I want pressure."

"I'll have to call D.C., speak to the old man himself, for that kind of clout."

"Do it!"

"Okay. Why the private investigator scam?"

"Two reasons. First, it's the only alternate credentials I have with me. Second, until I find out what this is all about, I doubt if the old man wants us involved officially."

"Reasonable. I'll move. It shouldn't take any more than an hour."

"Cut that in half if you can!"

Carter hung up, went into the street, and headed toward a bar he had already spotted. "Scotch, neat . . . a double."

He paid for the drink when it came, and carried it and his change to the pay phone in the corner.

"Klinikom-Charlottenburg, good afternoon."

"Give me the head nurse on Four East."

"One moment."

"Four East. This is Sister Gruber."

"Sister Gruber, this is Nick Carter. I accompanied Lisa Berrington to the hospital and signed her in."

"*Ja, ja,* Herr Carter."

"How is she?"

"Sleeping soundly now. We gave her another sedative."

"Did she awaken at all?"

"Only once, and I'm afraid she was still a bit hysterical. But I am sure she will be fine by tomorrow, mein Herr."

"Thank you. I'll call again later this evening."

He downed the scotch and went back across the street to SSD headquarters. On the second floor he parked on the same hard wooden bench that he had already warmed for almost two hours.

Twenty minutes later, Fräulein Metzger came at him down the hall like a one-woman panzer division.

"Follow me!" she grunted, whirled into reverse, and goose-stepped away.

"*Danke*," Carter replied with a wide smile as he followed her down the hall and into an office.

The hinges rattled when she slammed the door behind her.

The office was Spartan and drab, almost dingy. A well-worn oak desk held a telephone, a million uncoordinated papers, and about a hundred pipes. Two chairs and a wooden file cabinet of undeniable antiquity made up the rest of the furniture. The uncovered parquet floor was uneven and splintery, and the walls had been painted a nauseous green a decade or two earlier.

All in all, it was very shabby and somehow, to Carter, very un-German.

Carter was staring at a square patch on the wall where a picture or a calendar had once hung, when the door opened behind him.

"Carter?"

"Yes."

"I'm Vintner."

He was about six feet, a couple of inches shorter than Carter but twice as wide and all muscle. He was well dressed in a mussed summer suit that fitted his bulk perfectly, but he wore it with no flair. He looked "cop," the kind of man on whom clothes lost character and whose shoes, though polished, never seemed quite as bright as they should be.

"I speak German," Carter said in German.

"No shit. So do I," Vintner replied in New York-accented

English. "But ten-to-one my English is better than your German. Sit down."

Carter did, on the hard-bottomed, straight-backed chair, while Vintner slid onto the cracked leather one. The chief inspector shoved a pipe between his teeth and put fire to the bowl, eyeing Carter through the smoke screen he made.

His face had a battered appearance. His nose had been broken and poorly reset; there was a scar on his chin and a faint red line at his hairline where his gray hair refused to grow. All in all, it was a face that had seen the wars.

"Your English is good. I'd say aristocratic Queens."

"Princeton, Class of '43."

That was a grabber, and Carter didn't try to hide the reaction.

"My mother took me to the States two jumps in front of Hitler in '39."

"When did you come back to the fatherland?"

"In '45, with Patton. What do you want, Carter?"

"A helping hand. You give me one, I give you one. What do you say?"

"First of all, I say don't give me any bullshit. No P.I. in the world has the kind of clout that just got shoved up my ass. Who the hell are you?"

Carter weighed the situation, and the man, and made his decision. "Strictly between you and me?"

"I'll let you know after I know."

Carter nodded. He felt he was on equal footing with this man, and consequently in safe territory. He withdrew his oversize passport wallet and from a false side in the leather took out his true credentials.

Vintner took one look at them, passed them back, and leaned back in his chair. "Okay, what have you got?"

"You first," Carter said, lighting a cigarette to combat the pipe clouds more than anything.

"They both got it from a French F1, Tireur d'Elite, 7.62mm."

Carter whistled. "Sniper specialist."

Vintner nodded. "The woman died instantly. The officer,

Hans Erlichmann, took forty-five seconds from a scratch on his thigh."

"Cyanide?"

"Yes, they just confirmed it."

"What was the range?"

"Over four-hundred meters. We found the gun on top of the Insulaner. You know it?"

"I know it," Carter replied. "Any prints?"

"None. A couple of kids were messing around on a blanket on that side of the hill. They had sneaked up from the swimming pool. About the right time, a big guy in black leather and a helmet almost steps on them coming like hell down the hill."

"Did they see his face?"

Vintner shook his head. "He had his visor down. They saw him climb on a big BMW motorcycle and fly."

"But they didn't get the license number?"

"No way, too far away. But the boy identified the make, model, and year. He's got one himself. We've got the word out everywhere it matters. Chances are the bike was stolen within the last two weeks. Now you."

Carter told him about Lisa Berrington, the phone call, the rift in the Conway marriage, and his own reasons for being drawn into the fracas.

"Delaine Conway wasn't any more specific about what she was afraid of, was she?"

"No," Carter replied. "But I'll try to get a little more tomorrow. Lisa should be back to reality by then. What about Conway himself?"

Vintner shrugged. "Just cursory . . . grief and all that."

"Yeah," Carter said, noting the wryness in the man's voice. "When will you take his statement?"

"About noon tomorrow. He's at the Berlin Ambassador. I told him we could do it there."

"You mind if I sit in?"

"Suit yourself. Just remember, this is out of your line. I'm the cop."

Carter smiled. "No problem, you're the man. But we've

both got theories, haven't we?''

Suddenly the big chief inspector's granite face broke into a smile of its own. "Yeah, I imagine we do."

"All the more reason I'm a 'private detective' instead of connected." Vintner nodded, and Carter continued. "This kind of a hit would take a lot of money to finance, wouldn't it?"

"You know it would."

"I've got an appointment with a man at seven tonight who might help us in that area. In the meantime, do you have a copy of the television footage?"

"Of course."

He reached for the phone, and a minute later Fräulein Metzger entered. "Herr Carter would like to see the film," Vintner told her in clipped, commanding German.

"*Ja*, Herr Chief Inspector," she replied, looking at Carter through new eyes.

"Here's a number where you can reach me any time, day or night."

Carter pocketed the card. "I'm at the Victoria." He started after the woman, then paused in the doorway. "One more thing you could help me with . . ."

"Christ, man, you don't want much."

"Nothing major. What do you have on Oskar Hessling?"

Vintner's eyes narrowed in concentration, then he shrugged. "Not too much. He plays footsie with the other side now and then, so we have a suspect file on him. Basically, he's a local police problem."

"Could you get me access to that file?"

"I think so. Call me back in a couple of hours. Hessling's a fixer. You think he had something to do with this?"

"If he did, I don't know anything about it," Carter replied. "This is D.C. business."

"Call me."

"I will."

Carter watched the film clear through four times. There were several fine points of it that could substantiate Lisa's snap judgment that Delaine Conway, and not her illustrious husband, was the actual target.

Carter made mental notes of each of them to pass along to Vintner later, then left SSD headquarters to head for the Golden Calf.

Roscher Strasse was still relatively quiet at seven o'clock in the evening. The Ku'Damm and the streets leading from it, like Roscher Strasse, didn't really start swinging until the cats began to howl at around midnight.

That was the street, outside. Inside the bars and strip joints was another story, including the Golden Calf.

Two steps inside the door, an explosion of noise hit Carter full in the face. It was a combination of hard rock music, the cacophony of drinkers' shouted conversation, and the constant clinking of glasses and bottles behind a busy bar.

There were six women to every man. Most of them—the ones that were fully clothed—were bosomy and spangled. The waitresses and the five or six girls dancing on small stages around the room wore only one spangle and nothing else except spike heels or the female version of storm troopers' boots.

Carter got a few hundred appraisals as he moved through the clothed ones toward a slightly quieter area.

He yawned. It was the universal sign that he wasn't in the market. Their eyes looked for better game, and the bodies parted for him.

A clone of Maria Magdalena Metzger appeared the moment he sat down. Only this one was younger. And she was naked.

"*Ja?*"

"*Bier*," he said, holding up two fingers. "I have a friend coming."

She waddled away and came back quickly with two steins of suds. Carter paid her and sipped while he eyed the line along the bar. It was a game to pick out the real girls from the young boys dressed as girls.

He found six, and decided they were the ten, twelve, and two o'clock shows advertised on a huge wall poster.

"How's the clock-and-dagger business?"

Carter swiveled back around in his chair, smiled, and

accepted Jamil Erhanee's outstretched hand.

"Getting quieter every day."

"Untrue. You've aged. Thanks for the beer."

Jamil Erhanee was tall for an Indian, with wide shoulders, a thick chest, and no waist or hips. He could have been an athlete in his native Bombay if he hadn't decided that crime was a quicker road to riches.

It was tennis that got him to the United States and an education in international finance. As a sideline, he became a genius with a computer before the machines came into their own.

Soon after graduating from college, Erhanee drifted to England where he established strong underworld connections. From there it was onto Europe, where his genius was truly recognized. In no time he was laundering all kinds of funds all around the world. It was suspected that, at one time, Erhanee handled over three quarters of the funds being laundered and circulated internationally by the underworld.

But even that wasn't enough for the ambitious young Indian. He yearned for independence, so he became foolish. He saw the opportunity for the "big one." It was foolproof, he was sure. All he had to do was change a few wires here and there, make a telephone call or two to his own, privately installed computer modem, and he would beat the World Bank for a few million dollars.

He succeeded in pulling off the scam, but he got caught. They gave him twenty years. He had served five when Carter had him sprung to help on a mission. It was successful, and the Killmaster managed to get him a full parole.

"How goes it now, Jamil?"

"Boring," he said and shrugged, his sparkling white teeth bared in a gleaming smile. "But legitimate. I am in charge of security for World Bank computer systems. I make sure no one does what I did and gets away with it."

"That brings us down to business."

"Hessling?"

"Yeah, but something else first. Through your system, can you pipe into almost any bank, find out which way and where the cash is moving?"

"It's possible. Of course, in most cases, it is also very illegal."

"I know." Carter grinned. "That's why I'm asking you."

"Ah, Nick, you're a godsend!" Erhanee laughed.

"How so?"

"Because you make things happen. This will break the boredom! What do you want?"

"I want you to tap into Protec International Limited. I want to know about any big movement of cash in the last six months by the company and its president, Stephan Conway."

"That's the hotshot that almost bought it this afternoon," Erhanee replied, his face darkening beyond its already mahogany hue.

"That's right. Only his wife bought it instead. I want to know why, and you might give me the answer."

Carter could almost see the bells going off in the other man's agile brain.

"Sounds like hanky-panky. Hey, Nick, that's not your scene, dousing marital brush fires."

"It might be more than that. Conway had a high clearance with the Pentagon. He was making some very touchy, high-level electronics gear."

"Protec probably moves some pretty big bundles of cash around the world. What you need might be hard to pin down."

"I've got faith in you, Jamil. Also, can you go back to Day One on the wife, Delaine? Her maiden name was Berrington. Old Virginia money. I want to know what happened to it when she married Conway."

"That should be easy."

"More beer, mein Herr?"

Carter looked up to an arresting sight. "Uh . . ." He looked at Erhanee.

"Make mine schnapps. I get bloated on this stuff."

"Two schnapps, *bitte*."

"*Ja*."

Erhanee watched the young woman move away with appreciative eyes.

"You like 'em big?" Carter asked with a chuckle.

"Oh, yeah. Only trouble is, five years from now she'll look like a box and outweigh me by forty pounds."

The schnapps came and Carter paid her with a generous tip. As he dropped the money on her tray, he happened to glance around her. Near the bar he noticed an older woman conservatively dressed in a skirt and a cardigan sweater, which she held tightly together over the expanse of her bosom.

He would have thought nothing of it except for the fact that the woman was staring directly at them, and Carter could detect an almost morbid fear in both her manner and her eyes.

When their eyes met, the woman quickly turned and headed for the door that led to an adjoining hotel.

"Who is that woman?"

The waitress looked. "Fräulein Klammer. She is the manager. Why?"

"Just wondering why she was staring at us like that."

The girl laughed, making her bare breasts dance across the tray beneath them. "She probably thinks you're police," she said, and moved away.

"That'll be a cold day in hell," Erhanee said, laughing.

"What?"

"The day that anybody in this joint is afraid of the police!"

Carter shrugged off the odd feeling the staring woman had given him and leaned forward again, lowering his voice. "Okay, now Hessling."

The Indian sighed. "He's an enigma, Nick. You hear stories, but nothing concrete. He's slimy as hell, and has got his fingers in everything, but only he knows what. He's a loner. Probably got two, three hundred people under his thumb, but not a single one of them knows who the other one is."

"How can I get a line on him, particularly his deals with the East and anybody in the States?"

Erhanee thought for a moment, his narrow, handsome face screwed into rapt concentration, and then he smiled. "Voigt."

"Voigt who?"

"Hans-Otto Voigt. Anything shady or dirty that Hessling doesn't own or have his fingers in, Voigt does. They're the two powers around here. It's been almost war for years, but both of them are so powerful it's remained a standoff. If anybody knows more about Hessling than the police, it's probably Voigt. Call it the underworld form of industrial espionage."

"How can I get to this Voigt?"

"Pretty tough. He's semiretired, only handles the big deals. His son, Erich, takes care of the day-to-day business. The old man has a castle out on an island in the Havel. He hardly ever leaves it unless he goes south for the sun."

"See what you can set up for me."

"I'll try, but it might be rough. Got anything to use as bait?"

"I might have," Carter replied, checking his watch.

Vintner had said to call him in about two hours for the Hessling police file. It had been two and a half hours.

"Wait here a minute. I've got to make a phone call." He stopped by the bar and asked where the public pay phone was located.

"Up the stairs, by the desk," the barman replied, waving a hand toward the door where the frightened woman had disappeared.

Halfway up the stairs, he met her. She stood, arms folded beneath her bosom, feet planted wide apart. Even though the fear on her face was stronger than before, she was obviously blocking his path.

"What do you want?"

"To use the telephone, Fräulein Klammer."

"How do you know my name?"

"One of your girls told me."

"I know all the police on the Ku'Damm. You are not police."

"*Nein.*"

"You are SSD."

"*Nein.*"

"Why did you ask my name?"

"Curiosity."

"Liar," she hissed, and moved around him down the stairs.

Carter merely shrugged and moved on up the stairs to the phone.

"State Security."

"Chief Inspector Vintner, *bitte*."

"One moment, please." There was a brief pause and she was back. "Go ahead, mein Herr."

"Vintner."

"Carter. Were you able to get the file on Hessling?"

"Yes, but I doubt it will do you much good."

"How so?"

"He's dead. We got a call about an hour ago."

# EIGHT

Dieter Klauswitz dined in the large, rustically decorated dining room of the Metropol. He had meant to return immediately to his room but found himself instead wandering out onto Friedrich Strasse.

He would walk off the huge meal before returning to his room and attempting sleep.

To his right he saw the wall, eerily illuminated by sodium-vapor lights. It gave him an odd feeling. He had lived years in West Berlin, but this was the first time he had ever been in the Eastern sector.

Someone had once said, "If you want to find out what Berlin was like before the war, go visit the East."

It was true.

The pace was not as frantic, there were fewer cars and people on the streets, and everywhere were uniformed Vopos who seemed to watch every moving thing.

At the Unter den Linden, Klauswitz stopped and lit a cigarette. To his right, at the end of the two-hundred-foot-wide boulevard, was the Brandenburg Gate. He had never seen it up close, let alone from this side of the wall.

In its own way, the huge structure was a symbol of both the old and the new Germany. Klauswitz toyed with the idea of strolling down beneath the tall linden trees and taking one last, closer look. Then, out of the corner of his eye, to the left just south of the Unter den Linden, he saw the building.

97

It was formidable, a thick-walled, narrow-windowed fortress over four hundred feet long. It was the Soviet embassy.

Klauswitz retraced his steps back to the Metropol.

"From there he walked back to the hotel. He had one drink in the bar, a brandy, and went on up to his room."

Colonel Volatoy Balenkov nodded, his broad face impassive as he listened to the young lieutenant report on the movements of the American, David Klein.

"You got the passport from the concierge at the Metropol?"

"*Ja*, Herr Colonel. The experts have cleared it."

"Authentic?"

"Perfectly, Herr Colonel."

"Damn!" The colonel slammed the desk with one hand and stood. At the window he stared up Friedrich Strasse to the Metropol.

*What a mess*, he thought. Should he gamble that Oskar Hessling had told the truth?

Absently, his fingers ran over the ribbons above his left breast pocket on his gray tunic. The medals were impressive. Hero of the Soviet Union, the red and yellow Order of Lenin, the Order of the Red Banner, the maroon and pink for the capture of Berlin.

The list went on and on, and anyone who could read them would see that Volatoy Balenkov had had a distinguished military career.

But that wouldn't mean a thing in Moscow if he arrested an American businessman and had nothing to charge him with but the accusation of a West German criminal.

"What would you do, Lieutenant?"

The Stasis lieutenant's face came up sharply from the papers in his hands. It was not like a Russian, let alone a Russian colonel, to ask the opinion of an East German lieutenant.

"Based on the fact that Herr Hessling has never given us wrong information, I would hold him for questioning if nothing else."

Balenkov sighed and returned to his desk. "You have a point, Lieutenant. The trouble is . . . with Herr Oskar Hessling dead, we don't know what we are to arrest Klein for, or what to do with him if he is Klauswitz."

This was only partially true. Balenkov's suspicious, quick mind had been piecing together possibilities all day. For the past two hours he had been going over the files that their informant in the West German police had provided.

That same informant had told them of the day's chaotic events in the West, and less than fifteen minutes before, he had phoned over the news of Hessling's heart attack.

Now Balenkov lifted the Klauswitz file again. His eye scanned down it and, as it had so many times in the last hour, went right to the man's accomplishments before he had become a criminal.

He was a marksman, an expert in the rifle half of the biathlon. If David Klein were indeed Dieter Klauswitz, they may very well have their hands on a bombshell, the man who had attempted the assassination of the American, Stephan Conway.

Balenkov's thought processes had already gone one step further. If Oskar Hessling knew about this, he had probably set it up. Also, if he were betraying his shooter, he had something much more far-reaching—and much more profitable—on his mind.

The problem was, what the hell was it?

"The evidence has been placed in the hotel room?"

"*Ja,* Herr Colonel."

Balenkov rubbed his eyes until they were watery, and then looked up at the younger man.

"Arrest him."

Police inspector Klaus Reimer was a man who respected orders and authority. When word came from Horst Vintner and his own superior to answer all of Nick Carter's questions and cooperate with him, Reimer didn't question it.

"There is no doubt, Herr Carter . . . natural causes, a heart attack."

"But the scratches . . ."

"Made by a woman, and probably just before he died," Reimer replied.

"That would agree with the Italian's story."

"Yes."

"And if there was a woman, and a struggle," Carter said, "it could have brought on the heart attack?"

"Possibly."

"I would like to talk to the Italian."

"He is there, in the sitting room."

Carter moved through the door, nodded to a young officer who left at once, and turned to face Antonio Montanno.

He was about twenty, tall, broad-shouldered, with black curly hair and the chiseled good looks that Italian sculptors had glorified down through the ages.

"I'd like to hear your story," Carter said, lighting a cigarette.

"I've already told it ten times."

"Tell it again, to me."

Montanno sighed and began to mumble it out once more.

"Herr Hessling called the Golden Calf. He wanted me to drop by the house."

"Why?"

"To meet a woman."

"What woman?"

"I don't know. He didn't say."

"Why?"

The young man shrugged, his face flushing. "Who knows? I got here, rang the bell. No answer. I went back to the Calf and called. No answer. That's very unusual for Herr Hessling. I got worried. I came back, climbed the fence, let myself in through one of the windows, and found him. I was afraid—that's why I didn't call the police until this evening."

Carter crushed out the cigarette. "I don't think so. I think you're very handsome. I think Hessling sent for you because he wanted a homosexual affair. I think you turned him down. You fought. You scratched his face, and he had a heart attack and died. It's not exactly murder, but I think the police could make a manslaughter case out of it."

Montanno was laughing. "Hessling might have been a pervert, but he was no homosexual."

"Then why did he ask you over here in the middle of the night?"

"I told you, to meet a woman." His fingers were twisting against each other now, and his eyes were darting around the room, hitting everything but Carter's face.

"Just to meet her?"

He shrugged.

"Why don't you tell me, Tony? Reimer doesn't give a damn about you, and neither do I. We're after something a lot bigger."

Carter could see the turmoil in his young face. Suddenly the broad shoulders sagged and he sat back in the couch.

"All right. He wanted me to make love to this woman. Once or twice a month for the last year, he would call the Calf and have me come over. There would always be a girl. She and I would make love while Hessling watched."

"Did he pay you?"

"Yes. Always a hundred marks."

"And the woman?"

"Sometimes."

"What does that mean?"

Another shrug. "Most of the time they were street girls or from one of the clubs. They would always get a hundred marks, too. Other times . . . well, they were different."

"How?"

"Jesus, man . . ."

"How, Tony?"

"They . . . they hated it. It was like he was forcing them and I was raping them."

"Like he had something on them and this was how they kept him quiet?"

"Could be."

"Okay, Tony. Now, this morning . . . was there anything different about this morning?"

The young man thought for a minute, and nodded. "From the sound of it, I was going to get a lot more than a hundred marks. This one was something special. From the way he drooled on the phone, it sounded like she was a movie star or something.''

Carter stood. "Okay, kid. I think you're clean. Just tell Reimer everything you've told me, and I don't think you'll have any problems.'' He moved away, and then remembered. "What do you know about Gertrude Klammer?''

"Not much. She runs the Calf and the hotel, answers only to Hessling . . . *answered* only to Hessling.''

"Do you suppose Hessling had anything on her?''

Montanno smiled. This time it was genuine. "Hessling had something on everybody who worked for him. If it wasn't enough, he added bonus money to get them to do anything he wanted.''

"Could Gertrude Klammer have been the woman?''

"It's possible, I suppose, but I doubt it. Hessling liked them fairly young and beautiful.''

Carter nodded. "One more thing. Were there ever repeaters . . . the same girl or woman twice?''

"Never.''

Carter briefed Reimer and asked for a complete checkout on Gertrude Klammer, telling him about her odd behavior that night at the Golden Calf.

"But don't pick her up . . . not yet. Are the phones clean?''

"*Ja*, go ahead.''

He called the hospital. There was no change with Lisa Berrington.

Horst Vintner wasn't at SSD headquarters.

Erhanee picked up on the first ring when Carter dialed the private World Bank number the Indian had given him.

"You're burning the midnight oil.''

"Isn't that what you wanted?''

"How's it going?''

"Much better than I expected, but Protec is big. The printout will be longer than *War and Peace*, but I think I can have it for you by tomorrow afternoon.''

"Good. What about the other matter?''

"Just as I thought. No way to get to the old man unless you go through the son, Erich Voigt.''

"Where would I find him this time of night?"

"He has an office above a sleaze joint called the Bavarian. Number Ten Knesebeck Strasse, off the Ku'Damm."

"Is everything just off the Ku'Damm?"

"Everything sleazy is," Erhanee said with a chuckle. "According to my sources, this is about the time every night that Voigt counts the day's take."

"Thanks. See you."

Carter returned to Reimer. "You mentioned that you were going to keep Hessling's death under wraps for a few days?"

"If I can," the man said. "With him dead, it might be a good opportunity to scrape up a lot of dirt."

"What if Hans-Otto Voigt knew about it?"

Reimer's face screwed up into a look of pain. "He'd mobilize his troops to take over Hessling's territory as soon as we backed out."

"Would you mind if I tell him?"

Reimer smiled. "Will it do you some good?"

"It might."

"Go ahead. Voigt will find it out before the papers get it anyway. Sad as it is, he's probably got someone in the department."

"And along with the Hessling file, can you get me everything on Voigt?"

"*Ja*, I'll send it over to your hotel in the morning."

"*Danke* . . . a lot."

Carter headed for the door. The little man in the back of his mind was pounding, telling him that there was a connection between the try on Conway, the death of Delaine, and Oskar Hessling.

Dieter Klauswitz was dozing in a chair by the window, the radio a soft hum behind him, when the knock came on the door.

"Yes?"

"Security, Herr Klein. Could we speak to you for a moment?"

There was a second of panic when he first leaped for the door. But he quickly calmed. He was an American businessman. Everything was completely in order.

He opened the door.

There were two of them, in plain clothes. Over their shoulders he saw two Vopos with their banana-clipped rifles across their chests. That was nothing to get alarmed about. They were everywhere, and they probably slept with their rifles.

"What can I do for you?"

"Routine, Herr Klein. Could I see your papers, please?"

They moved forward into the room without being asked, forcing Klauswitz to move with them.

"My passport and entrance visa are at the desk."

"We know that, Herr Klein. Could we see your currency declaration, please?"

"Of course." He fished it from his briefcase and passed it over.

The man perused it, then moved to the bed. "Would you lay out your currency so we may compare it, please?"

Klauswitz stayed calm. Everything was covered. There was nothing left to chance. He was an American. His passport was authentic, issued directly through the office of an American senator. He could even go screaming to the American embassy.

"There you are." He laid out all his bills: British pounds, American dollars, West German marks, what was left of the twenty-five East German marks he had exchanged at Checkpoint Charlie, and his change. "You are Vopo?"

"Stasis," came the reply as the man meticulously counted the money.

*State security police*, Dieter thought. *What are they looking for?*

"This is all your currency, Herr Klein?"

"Of course."

The second man went to work on the two bags and their contents.

"See here, I am an American—"

"Simply routine, Herr Klein," said the money counter as he moved to the closet and began patting down the two extra suits.

Suddenly he stopped, took one of the suit jackets off its hanger, and carried it to the bed. With a penknife, he began to cut the lining.

"See here! You can't just come in here and do this! How dare . . .!" Klauswitz stopped in mid-sentence, his face ashen.

Pouring out of the lining of the jacket were East German marks, all in high denominations.

"It is illegal to bring Eastern marks into the German Democratic Republic, Herr Klein. Since, according to your currency declaration, you couldn't have bought these since your arrival . . ."

Klauswitz didn't speak. He knew it would do no good. It was a frame. The marks had been planted. But why?

"You are under arrest, Herr Klein. Will you come with us, please?"

The Bavarian was not much different from the Golden Calf, just bigger. The girls were just as fleshy, the customers just as loud, and the male help just as mean.

"Scotch, neat."

The barman, a sallow-faced man with no neck, poured from the bottle. "Five marks."

Carter put a twenty on the bar. "Keep it. I'd like to see Erich Voigt."

"He's not in tonight."

"I think he is, upstairs counting his ill-gotten gains."

The barman turned laser-beam eyes on Carter. "Police?"

"No, just a concerned citizen."

"Why don't you drink your drink and find another bar?"

"Why don't you go and tell Voigt a very important man wants to see him?"

The barman reached for him, but Carter was faster. He threw the scotch in the man's eyes and pushed him.

"What's the trouble here?"

He was a mountain in a tacky tuxedo right at Carter's elbow. He had a flat face, pig eyes, and arms as big as Carter's legs.

"No trouble. Who are you?"

"I am the man who stops trouble."

"Good, Bismarck. Then tell your boss an American, Nick Carter, wants to talk to him about Oskar Hessling."

The giant hands were coming up as Carter spoke. Now they stopped, and his face, if possible, became thoughtful. "Hessling?"

"That's right. I think Herr Voigt would be very angry if I didn't see him." Carter could read the man's indecision. "Move!"

Bismarck moved, and Carter turned back into the barman's boiling face.

"Son of a bitch," the man hissed.

"Now, now," Carter replied, and poured himself a fresh drink.

He was just finishing it when he saw the giant motioning to him from a small hallway in the rear of the room. Carter shouldered his way through the crowd and joined him.

"This way."

They went up the stairs, and Carter entered a shiny chrome-and-glass office that was nothing like the joint down below. A short, thin, blond-haired man with a pug nose, drawn mouth, and small, sharp brown eyes sat behind a huge desk.

He looked up as Carter entered, curled his lip, and went back to the stacks of money spread out in front of him.

"Erich Voigt?"

"That's who you wanted to see. Who the hell are you?" He had a rough, gravelly voice that didn't match his size, and he was wearing about five grand worth of suit and jewelry.

"I need some information."

"So do I. Who are you?"

"Carter, American, private detective."

"I don't talk to detectives, private or otherwise."

"Suits me. It's your father I want to talk to anyway. I always believe in going right to the top."

The scowl was real, and his voice, when he spoke again, got even lower and rougher. "You saw my manager downstairs and my bouncer?"

"Yeah."

"Together they weigh over five hundred pounds."

"So?"

"So I think you'd better go before I have them break your arms and legs."

"You don't want to hear about Hessling?"

"What . . . that he's dead? I knew it five minutes after the body was discovered."

That was like a hard right in the gut, but Carter didn't flinch. "You're connected better than I thought."

Voigt finished playing with his money, snapped a rubber band around a stack of bills, and laid an ugly-looking Walther on the desk between them.

"You have five seconds to get out of here before I shoot a would-be thief."

Carter stood. "Tell Hans-Otto that the wisest thing he will do in the next few days is see me."

The little man was reaching for the gun when Carter went out the door. Downstairs, the barman was talking rapidly on the phone. Bismarck was nowhere in sight.

Carter stepped out onto the street, turned right, went about ten yards, and froze. It was empty. For two solid blocks, there wasn't a soul. It was the high part of the night. There should have been tourists and locals, hookers and freaks moving and laughing between the bars.

There was nothing, no one, not a sound. It was like a war zone just before the battle starts.

He moved on a few more paces, and heard feet hit the street behind him. It was like a signal. They came out of darkened doorways in front of him, Bismarck and two more almost as beefy. Carter threw a quick glance over his shoulder and saw the barman coming at him with a sap.

The sap was a bad lead. Carter dodged, and it went harmlessly past his back. The Killmaster hit the barman in the throat with a left that traveled only twelve inches.

The man took a short backward step, grunting and fighting for air. Carter kicked him in the gut and then got him a second time in the chest. He went sailing into one of the others.

That left Bismarck and his other pal. Carter started to spin to meet them, but he was too late.

A pair of fists like iron caught him square in the middle of the back, sending him to the ground. He could see the barman still lying on the ground a few feet away, still clutching his throat and belly, but the other three were up and ready to go.

They began putting the boots to him, and Carter covered up.

"Watch his head!"

"Yeah, leave him breathing . . . don't kill him!"

*Bastards*, Carter thought, and did a three-eighty spin on his hip, with his legs out. He caught two of them and leaped to his feet.

Bismarck was coming at him, still on his feet. Both hands were held out in front of him, the fingers rigid and the thumbs tucked in behind them.

He made a leap toward Carter, his right hand swinging down in a slashing motion. The Killmaster moved in under it and kicked him hard in the left shin. The grunt from his thick lips was pure agony.

All pain is pain, and Carter was feeling his share of it from their boots. But bone pain is something else again.

Bismarck hopped for a second, and that gave Carter time to kick him in the other shin.

The other two were coming on again. The Killmaster side-kicked one of them in the gut, but the other one rang his bell with a hard right to the side of the head. Carter faked a go-down, and caught him with an elbow in the testicles when he fell for it.

Then he went for the moaning Bismarck. Carter knew he had to make it fast now. His back, his ribs, and his head ached like the end was close. He knew he couldn't take much more.

He put two into Bismarck's gut with all the strength left in his arms, and grabbed hold of the man's left wrist. Carter wound his arm up behind the man's back and turned him.

Then he got a firm grip on the back of his neck and, with his other hand in his belt, ran him across the sidewalk.

The giant's head slammed into the brick wall with a dull thud, and Carter let him slip to the cement.

The barman was up, groggy and clutching his throat, but coming on. Carter stepped forward and kicked his legs from beneath him. He went down with him, slightly faster, so his knee was waiting for the big man's gut.

By the time he was sprawled on the sidewalk on his back, there wasn't much fight left in him.

"What's your name?"

Silence, hate in his eyes, blood dribbling from the side of his mouth.

Carter curled his fingers in the side of his hair and bounced the back of his head on the sidewalk a couple of times.

"Speak to me."

"Dirk . . ." he gagged.

"Okay, Dirk, after you clean this mess up, you go back in and tell little Erich that this is just the beginning. Hear me?"

Blink. Gag.

The Killmaster dribbled his head a few more times on the concrete. When the gags sounded like "Yes," he stopped.

"Tell him I'm at the Victoria. If I don't get word by early morning that I see Hans-Otto, it's war."

Carter staggered down the street and out on the Ku'Damm. It was a half block to a taxi stand, and he almost didn't make it.

The driver calmly surveyed him. "Hospital?"

"The Victoria."

"You're sure, mein Herr?"

"I'm sure. But if you know about a rear entrance, that would help."

The lights in his room were on, and Lisa Berrington was sitting on the side of the bed.

"Good God, what happened to you?"

"What the hell are you doing here?"

"First things first."

"I tried to prove how macho I am on the wrong side of town. Now you. How did you get in here?"

"The maid. She thinks we're having an affair."

"And out of the hospital?"

"I woke up and was rational. A policeman named Bruchner from the SSD came and took my statement. When it was over, I demanded he spring me."

"Are you all right?"

"Better than you. Here, let me help you with that."

She helped him with his jacket, set him on the bed, and poured two stiff drinks. As he sipped his, she started peeling away his clothes.

"Mind?"

"No. Silly question. How do you feel?"

"You asked me that already."

"I'm asking again."

"A little queasy when I think on it too much. Mostly angry. Want to bring me up to date?"

He did, as she finished getting him almost naked and then started doing marvelous things to his sore muscles with her hands.

"That should prove it, shouldn't it? That Stephan hired someone to kill my sister?"

"Circumstantial," Carter growled. "We need more. A motive. A who. The killer, so far, has got away clean."

"God, your whole body is turning black and blue."

"Whatever you're doing, it's helping."

She had moved away from the bed. Now she was back, her hands at it again. He lay with his eyes closed. The next moment he winced and nearly cried out as probing fingers found the ache in the bruised muscles of his back.

"Ow, enough!" he cried.

"Don't," she said when he tried to push her away. "Just relax. I don't think there is anything broken."

"Not yet!"

"Shhh."

Carter sighed and did manage to relax. She was good. Her massaging fingers seemed able to reach deep to the core of his aches and soreness. There was an exquisite agony, but in its wake a soothing calmness spread through him.

After that single, feeble protest, Carter felt himself grow limp, and he submitted without resistance to the treatment. He could hear her voice drone in a steady monotone, but he scarcely knew what she was saying.

He felt her hands peeling off his last piece of clothing, his shorts. Then she was working on the ache where pummeling fists had punished his kidneys. In long, soothing strokes, her strong fingers ran up the column of his back, across his tortured shoulders, down the slope of his rib cage. He could feel the agony slipping away, to be replaced by a delicious sense of well-being and then, unbelievably, a miraculous resurgence of strength.

"Thanks," he gasped finally. "You're one hell of a nurse!"

"Oh, I almost forgot. When the SSD officer, Bruchner, left me off . . ."

"Yeah?"

"A woman—a big, blond woman—from his office was waiting in the lobby for you. She left these."

Carter took the two manila envelopes from Lisa's hands and ripped them open. He quickly went through the Voigt file.

"Hand me a pad out of that briefcase, will you?"

She did. "Important?"

"Very." He told her in no uncertain terms just who Hans-Otto Voigt was, and how much clout the old man had. "I think he can come up with answers better and much faster than I or the police can. I just have to get to him."

"Is that so difficult?"

"Very, but I think I've got a way." Carter managed to roll his feet over the side of the bed and then stood with a groan.

Only then did he realize that he was totally naked. "Um, this is a bit awkward . . ."

"Not really." She smiled. Her fingers went to work on her dress.

"I could put on a robe."

"I'd rather you didn't," she said, her smile broadening as she shrugged out of the dress. She stood in a half-slip and bra, boldly appraising him. The breasts that swelled her bra to bursting hung heavy and taut behind black lace. "Better?"

"Almost."

She was working the half-slip downward as he made his way to the phone.

He got the AXE hot-line operator on the line, and gave her Marty Jacobs's name and a code-red designation. She went to scrambler and came back on in seconds. "Mr. Jacobs isn't here, sir."

"I figured he wasn't. Put me through to his home."

"Yes, sir."

A very sleepy voice mumbled something like, "Yeah, who is it?"

"Marty, this is Carter."

"Christ, Nick, it's three o'clock in the morning!"

"The fight for freedom never sleeps. Got a pencil?"

"Gimme a minute." He was back in ten seconds. "Shoot."

"I want to put the squeeze on Hans-Otto Voigt and his little boy Erich."

"What kind of a squeeze?"

Carter told him, and then read his own notes scribbled from the file. "How many men do you have?"

"Six in-house, and I can get about fifteen more."

"That should be enough."

"Nick, are you nuts? You want to start World War Three in West Berlin, let alone what the police will do to us if something goes wrong!"

"I'll take care of the cops. You just put three teams together. Start with his morning couriers taking the operating capital to the illegal casinos. Also, hit four or five of his bookmakers and the safe in the Bavarian."

"You're out of your goddamned mind!"

"I know, but I'll lay you twenty-to-one it'll work. I'll let you know first thing in the morning when to move."

"I'll get right on it."

"You're a good man, Jacobs. *Ciao*."

Carter dropped the pad and files on the telephone stand, stood, and turned to face Lisa. She had stretched out on the bed, naked.

"Aren't you taking an awful chance?" she asked.

"Yeah, but you fight fire with fire."

"Come, kiss me."

"You sure?"

"I'm sure. I don't want to sleep alone. If I'm with you, I won't dream. I'll have something to hang on to."

Carter made it to the bed, where she moved over and made room for him. She turned and lay sideways on the bed, facing him, her weight on an elbow stretched across his body, her head propped in her hand. He felt her solid, warm breasts settle on his chest. Doubling the pillow under his head so he could get a better look at her, he ran a hand through her hair. It was wet from her exertions over him.

"He did it, didn't he?" she whispered softly.

Carter nodded. "I think so. The shooter was good, too good to miss. I don't think he missed. I think Voigt can tell me for sure, and if Hessler hired the shooter, I think we've got a motive."

She trembled. "The bastard."

Carter snapped off the light and touched her shoulder gently. She came against him willingly, wantonly.

"You're sure?" he rasped into the side of her neck.

"I'm sure," she murmured.

Carter felt her move over him, felt the warmth of her lips and then her whole mouth.

"Relax," she said. "Remember, I know exactly what I'm doing."

# NINE

"We have worked him in teams all night, Herr Colonel."

Balenkov scraped a little more beard off the right side of his face before he spoke. "And he has told you nothing beyond his name, rank, and serial number."

"What, Herr Colonel?"

"Nothing. What does he say?"

"He claims to be what his papers say he is, and he demands to call his embassy."

The colonel nodded at his own reflection in the mirror and wiped the lather from his face. "It figures. It will be impossible to trip him up. What he has is too strong."

The lieutenant held the older man's uniform tunic. "Should we employ persuasion?"

"We may have to, but only as a last resort. No, I think in Herr Klein/Klauswitz's case, we shall try reason."

Balenkov didn't elaborate, and the Stasis lieutenant didn't question him further. The two men left the Russian's rather Spartan apartment and descended to the waiting Chaika.

"Your office, Comrade Colonel?"

"*Nyet*. Kempelstoff."

The high-domed black car pulled from the curb onto Karl Marx Strasse, heading for Lichtenberg and East Berlin's top security prison.

The lieutenant started to make conversation, but Balenkov quieted him with a slight wave of his hand. The colonel's mind was working, going over every facet of information they had gleaned on the previous day's events in the West.

He already had a theory that had been partially confirmed by Moscow the previous evening. But putting the rest of it together was a puzzle of several pieces.

Eventually he pulled memos, notes, files, and a pad from his briefcase. Diligently he went through every scrap of information and jotted more notes as he read.

By the time they reached the prison, Balenkov was fairly sure he could make a reasonable case.

Carter managed to shower, shave, dress, and slip from the room without awakening Lisa Berrington.

He stopped by the desk on the way to the dining room. "Any calls or messages for Room Seven-fourteen, Carter?"

"*Nein, mein Herr.*"

Over toast, juice, and coffee, Carter jotted down questions he would like to have the answers for from Stephan Conway. It was almost nine when he paid his check and returned to the front desk.

"Still nothing, Herr Carter."

"*Danke.*" He turned, and practically ran into Bruchner.

"Inspector Vintner is in the car."

"I'll only be a second," Carter replied. "One call."

The AXE operator hit the scrambler connect the instant he mentioned his name, and seconds later a raspy-voiced Marty Jacobs was on the line.

"I hope *you* got some sleep."

"A little, not much," Carter replied, remembering the almost insatiable demands Lisa had made on his sore body earlier. "How far along are we?"

"Set. Of course we'll have to be a little circumspect in the daylight hours. The real action won't start until tonight. That is, if it's a go."

Carter could tell from the nervousness in the man's voice that he hoped Carter's answer would be negative.

"It's a go . . . . all the way."

"Oh, Christ."

"Cheer up, Marty. Whatever your boys get, we'll donate to your favorite charity."

"You know, of course, that we are breaking the laws of a friendly country."

"So are the Voigts. I'll ring you for a progress report this afternoon."

Besides the driver and Bruchner, there was a young blond stenographer who looked all business. Carter was introduced as he slid into the back seat, and Vintner answered the Killmaster's eyeball question with a nod: it was okay to talk.

"Anything new?"

"Damned little," the chief inspector replied. "The Fl was ripped off from a French military armory in Marseilles. We did a roundup, but so far all the pros we've brought in for questioning have tight alibis. I think what we need is something that will shake the street up, get some answers."

Carter smiled. "I think I have a way of doing that that you don't have."

He elaborated, and then held his breath until a broad smile spread across Vintner's face. "I'll give Reimer the word from the ambassador to have his people go blind."

"I think it will work," Carter said.

"So do I. Of course, I haven't heard a word you've said."

"Of course." Carter handed the man the list of questions he had made over breakfast. "I'd rather have you ask those. I think it better, at this point, that Conway not know who I am."

"Herr Vintner?" It was Bruchner from the front seat.

"*Ja?*"

"The radio . . . evidently a terrorist attack in the drive of a private residence in Grunewald. Two vehicles were bombed, no one injured."

Vintner started to reach for the radiophone connection in the back seat, and suddenly stopped. "Find out who owned the vehicles!"

"*Ja.*" Bruchner went back to his headset, and seconds later he turned toward the rear seat. "A late-model Mercedes and a new Rolls-Royce, both registered to Erich Voigt."

"Tell the section police to handle it."

"*Ja, mein Herr.*"

Vintner turned to Carter and grinned. "Your people don't waste any time."

"Herr Klein, I am Colonel Volotoy Balenkov."

Dieter Klauswitz ignored the outstretched hand and rose to his full height. His eyes were watery and red from lack of sleep, but there was grim determination in his face.

"Colonel, as an American citizen I demand that I be allowed to contact my embassy."

"In due time, Herr Klein." Balenkov sat and began arranging his papers.

"I also demand an inspection of my jacket."

"Your jacket?"

"Yes. I believe the lining of my jacket was opened, the GDR notes inserted, and the jacket resewn."

"Who would do that, Herr Klein?"

"Probably the maids at the hotel, at your order."

"I see you have very little respect for us, Herr Klein."

"I have none at all."

One eyebrow arched sharply. "I must remind you where you are . . ."

"You need hardly do that. I've known I was in a police state from the moment I passed through Checkpoint Charlie."

"Why did you enter East Germany, Herr Klein?"

"I have a ticket on Aeroflot for London."

"There are flights to London from West Berlin."

"I was curious."

"I see." The man was good, Balenkov thought; he bluffed well. The colonel only hoped he could *be* bluffed. "Please sit down, mein Herr. I wish you to read something, and then perhaps we can discuss a theory of mine."

Reluctantly, the blond man sat down and accepted the paper-clipped file folder. Balenkov watched his face closely, and cursed to himself when there wasn't a blink, an eyebrow raised, or a discernible change of expression.

The file was the West Berlin police dossier on Dieter Klauswitz.

"Interesting, but what does it have to do with me?"

"Perhaps nothing, but three things in that file, despite the fact that Klauswitz is a known criminal, intrigue me. Do you know what the biathlon is?"

"I believe it is an athletic event that includes cross-country skiing and shooting."

"Shooting with a rifle, yes. You will note from the file that Klauswitz is a master marksman. You will also notice that during his brief military career he was stationed in Stuttgart, and after his military service, attended the American University in Munich. I suspect Herr Klauswitz's English is as good as mine . . . or yours."

"I have met several Germans who spoke perfect English."

"Of course," the colonel replied. "Bear with me, Herr Klein; I am putting something together. Are you aware that an assassination attempt was made on an American businessman in West Berlin yesterday?"

"No, I was not aware of that."

"No matter. The man wasn't killed. His wife and a police officer were."

"Look here, I'm tired of all this—"

"Herr Klein, shut up." Balenkov went to his notes. "We have reason to believe that one Oskar Hessling hired Dieter Klauswitz to commit this crime. I received a memo from First Directorate, KGB Moscow, last evening that connects Herr Klein to Oskar Hessling. It seems that Hessling attempted to blackmail Herr Klein a few years ago. We think that this attempted assassination might well be a further attempt at blackmail."

"I ask you again, what in God's name has all of this got to do with me?"

"A great deal, I think, Herr Klein. From the time the shooting took place until you came through the wall was exactly one hour and fifteen minutes. Our people in the West have also made discreet inquiries this morning with officials of Mockdendorf Limited. They have indeed done business with Herr David Klein recently, but only by phone and telex. According to them, David Klein has not been in Germany personally for over a year.''

Balenkov paused, studying his quarry. It was slight, but the signs were there: a subtle pinch around the mouth, the barely perceptible sag in the otherwise square shoulders, the quivering of the nostrils.

The colonel could sense it. He almost had his man.

''And there was, of course, the phone call from Herr Hessling the morning before you came over.''

''What?''

''Oh, yes, Herr Hessling and I have done quite a bit of business in the past.''

Balenkov slid a small cassette recorder-player from his briefcase and punched the Play button.

''*Stasis, Corporal Kleimann.*''

''*Colonel Balenkov, bitte.*''

''*Bitte.*''

''*Balenkov.*''

''*Guten Abend, mein Herr.*''

''*Ah, Hessling. I was wondering when you were going to call. What do I get for my little favors?*''

''*As yet, Colonel, I am not sure. But the prospect for reward is great. Sometime in the late afternoon, today, an American, David Klein, will check into the Metropol.*''

''*Yes?*''

''*His real name is Dieter Klauswitz. He's a West German, currently out on parole and awaiting trial for robbery. That should be enough to hold him for a few days, shouldn't it?*''

''*More than enough. But why?*''

''*I must make a contact or two on Tuesday. I'll call you that evening and let you know what to do with him, and how great both our rewards will be. Auf Wiedersehen, Colonel.*''

''*Wiedersehen, Herr Hessling.*''

Balenkov pushed the Stop button and looked up at the man across the table. The fair face was gray now, and he was holding his temples with his hands.

''And so, Dieter, you see, you were betrayed from the

beginning. And I think we know why. Your instructions were not to kill Stephan Conway, were they?''

"No.''

"It was the woman all along, wasn't it?''

"*Ja,*" Klauswitz replied in German. "*Der Fell Schweinhund!*''

"I completely agree, Herr Klauswitz, with your opinion of Herr Hessling. Now, suppose we start from the beginning, the very beginning, including all the names you know.''

"What do I get out of it?''

Balenkov shrugged. "I suppose you have already arranged another passport in another name in England, since David Klein actually exists?''

"*Ja.* I was going on to Portugal, and then to Argentina.''

"Yes, I'm sure you would have made many friends there,'' Balenkov replied drily. "I see no reason that, once we have what we want, you cannot continue on your journey.''

"How can I trust you?''

"Actually, you have no choice. But I will say this: we don't want the scandal of an assassin passing through East Germany. The quicker you are on your way, the better for us.''

Klauswitz sighed. "May I have a cigarette?''

"Of course.'' Balenkov pushed an open pack across the table and punched Record on the machine.

Dieter Klauswitz talked for two hours and seven minutes. At the end of that time, Colonel Balenkov had filled in everything from the other side of the coin—Hessling's side—that Klauswitz couldn't know. He figured it should be an easy matter to locate the other woman.

"Very good, Dieter,'' he said finally, gathering up everything and putting it in his briefcase. "You may rest now, and let's hope we have you on your way soon.'' He met the lieutenant in the hallway. "Has she arrived?''

"*Ja,* Herr Colonel, about a half hour ago. She is in the sixth-floor lounge.''

Balenkov took the elevator to the sixth floor and walked

down the hall to the ranking officers' lounge.

He knew of her reputation and had heard of her beauty, but the reality of it struck him when at last he met her face to face.

"Colonel Balenkov?"

"*Da.*"

"I am Colonel Anna Palmitkov. Shall we get right down to business?"

Stephan Conway was a mixture of grief, stricken husband, Texas-style good-old-boy bluff and bravado, and wily businessman.

Carter had scarcely shaken the man's hand when he recognized why the media was dancing to Conway's tune. He was big, handsome, suave, and crude, all at the same time. He cussed well, and told anecdotes with a mix of down-home wit and parish-house piety.

He also managed to interject his "dear sweet wife" into every third sentence.

"I want the maniac who did this, Inspector, and I want his ass nailed to the wall!"

It had been a half hour since they had entered the Berlin Ambassador suite, and Vintner had, as yet, not been able to ask one question.

Besides the inspector, the steno, Carter, and Conway, there was an entire phalanx of the great man's hangers-on, six men and three women. Conway hadn't bothered to introduce them beyond a wave and a perfunctory "part of my staff."

The men could be grouped into the attorney-accountant categories. Two of them were American, the other four German. Two of the women were American-type secretaries, clean-cut, wholesome, and studious, as befit those who worked near the throne.

It was the third woman who interested Carter, and from the way Vintner's steno kept throwing quick sidelong glances, she was curious as well. Curious, or in awe.

Carter guessed the latter, and could see why.

He had barely caught her name, Ursula Rhinemann, but he couldn't miss her presence. No one, even in a room of one hundred beautiful women, would miss it.

She was a tall, statuesque woman in her late twenties or early thirties. She wore her dark hair short, with easy curls at the sides framing an exquisitely featured face set in a mask of seriousness. Her eyes, staring intently at the questioning Vintner, were level, cool, and of an indeterminate color beneath long, darkly mascaraed lashes.

She had the kind of haunting face and sensuous figure that drew and held men's eyes. Carter was no different.

Only when the voices of Vintner and Stephan Conway were raised in anger was the Killmaster's concentration drawn back to the two men.

"As mundane as this questioning may seem to you, Herr Conway, I assure you it is not. Now, will you please tell me about the blackmail attempt?"

Conway furrowed his wide brow and looked to his attorneys. There must have been some imperceptible nod of agreement, because he started to talk.

"When I was a student I joined a couple of left-wing organizations. It was one of those idealistic college things," he said with a shrug. "When I found out that they were Communist connected, I got out. It's as simple as that."

Vintner nodded. "But obviously someone remembered."

"Yes. I was contacted by a man in San Francisco and shown some petitions I had signed years ago. I was told the material would be suppressed if I agreed to sell certain electronics technology and equipment to a firm here in West Germany."

"And?"

"And I told them to go to hell."

"So those petitions were given to the American FBI."

"Yes."

"And you were investigated?"

"I was, and cleared. I don't see what this has to do with the attempt on my life."

"Perhaps nothing, perhaps something," Vintner said evenly. "Do you know of anyone who would want your wife killed?"

"Of course not! She didn't have an enemy in the world."

"But there were threats against your life."

"Yes."

"When?"

"The morning we got to Berlin."

"How? . . . Letters? Someone came to you?"

Conway hesitated. Again a quick look at his people. Vintner didn't catch it. He was looking down at his notes. Carter did. The eye contact was directly with Ursula Rhinemann.

"No, it was a phone call, here at the hotel."

"And what did they want?"

"The same thing, electronics. I think it's the damned Commies."

Vintner shifted gears. "I have a statement here from your sister-in-law, Ms. Lisa Berrington, that states that you and your wife were on the verge of divorce."

"Preposterous!" Conway thundered, jumping to his feet. "Lisa's a bitch! She has never liked me, and has always done everything in her power to split us up! Oh, Delaine and I had our arguments, but what couple doesn't?"

"I see." Vintner sighed. He gathered his papers and stood. "When will you be leaving Germany, Herr Conway?"

"I know my dear wife would want me to go on with my work. I am scheduled to speak in Munich in four days. I shall probably leave Berlin that morning." ,

"Thank you for your cooperation."

The steno was already out the door. Carter fell in step behind her, and then stopped.

"Herr Conway, I wonder if I could ask you one more question?" Carter spoke English with a heavy German accent.

"What is it?"

"Do you know a man by the name of Oskar Hessling?"

The man was a good actor, but the question had come out of left field, a direction he had not fully prepared to defend.

There was ever so slight a twitch at the right eye, a little breath, and the start of another look at the woman, which he arrested just in time.

"No, I've never heard the name."

"I see. *Danke*."

Vintner was the first to speak in the elevator. "What do you think?"

"I think he's guilty as sin," Carter replied.

Vintner nodded. "So do I, but it will be hard to prove without the shooter or the man who hired him. It's a pretty elaborate scam just to get rid of one's wife. Almost unbelievable."

"I have a theory," Carter said. "The blackmail was for real. Conway wants to get rid of his wife, so he used it to promote rumors that he's about to be hit, but the target is really the wife."

"Like I say," Vintner replied, "pretty elaborate and farfetched. *And* damned hard to prove."

"Maybe." Carter turned to the blond stenographer. "I saw you staring at the tall, dark-haired woman. Do you know her?"

The girl nodded. "Her name is Ursula Rhinemann. A few years ago her picture was on every magazine cover in Germany. She was a fashion model. She is even more beautiful now."

"What's her connection with Conway?"

Vintner consulted a printout of Protec's administrative staff. "She's head of public relations for Europe."

"That's a hell of a job for a fashion model," Carter quipped.

Vintner shrugged. "Not if she's got brains as well as beauty. It might be a plus. What are you thinking?"

"An old-fashioned, very simple triangle."

"With Ursula Rhinemann as the other woman?" Vintner said, his bushy eyebrows arching.

"You saw her. What do you think?"

Vintner nodded. "I'll put a team on her."

Bruchner awaited them at the car, smiling. "We've got the motorcycle! A young punk was picked up for speeding on Bismarck Strasse. He admits stealing it from a garage in Wedding."

"Any chance he's our shooter?"

Bruchner shook his head. "None. He's a petty thief, long record, but not capable of this. A team has already interrogated the neighbors around Wiebe Strasse. An old man remembers the biker going into the garage on the BMW and coming back out in a white Mercedes."

"License number? Description of the driver?"

Bruchner's face fell. "No tag number, and all he remembers is that the driver was blond."

"At least it's a start," Carter said, crawling into the car. "Drop me at Tessiner Stuben. I have a meeting with a man who might have some answers."

# TEN

"Fräulein Klammer?"

"*Ja.*" Gertrude Klammer's palms, holding the door open a crack, were sweating. This woman wasn't from the Ku'Damm, but she didn't look like police, either.

"I would like to talk to you, Fräulein Klammer."

"I am busy now."

The white Mercedes was due back at Tegel. She hadn't gotten the call to pick it up. She didn't know where to pick it up. She didn't know what to do. Was this woman from Europa?

"I would like to talk to you about a white Mercedes, Fräulein Klammer."

Gertrude Klammer's face went as white as the car. "Are you from Europa?"

"No, Fräulein Klammer. I have something I want you to read."

A paper was passed through the crack. Gertrude read it and sagged against the wall, letting the door swing wide.

"*Mein Gott . . .*"

The woman had entered and closed the door behind her. "I want you to sign that paper, Fräulein Klammer."

"But this is a confession! It says I helped an assassin escape!"

"You did, Fräulein Klammer, when you rented the Mercedes and left it in the Wiebe Strasse garage."

"Who are you, police?"

"No. It doesn't matter who I am. We have this knowledge, and we have uses for it. I assure you, Fräulein Klammer, we have no intention of using it against you."

"But I didn't even know it was Oskar Hessling who hired me!"

"We know that. Just sign, Fräulein Klammer. And if you should want to leave Berlin . . ." The woman placed a stack of one-thousand-mark notes and a pen on the table. "Sign, Fräulein Klammer."

Gertrude Klammer could feel her pulse racing. "I have no choice, do I?"

"None. If you don't, a copy of that will be mailed to the SSD. It will only be a matter of time."

Gertrude sat and, with a quivering hand, signed the paper.

She barely felt the thin piano wire touch her throat before she was gasping out her last breath.

The restaurant was rosy in the glow of the midafternoon sun. It smelled of fresh flowers and good food. Carter ordered a drink, a beer, and a double order of turbot with leeks *en papillote*.

He was two fingers down on his drink when a very weary Jamil Erhanee slid into the opposite chair and dropped a six-inch bundle in front of Carter.

"You've been busy."

Erhanee sipped his beer. "Keeping the modems hot."

"Boil it down for me."

The Indian took a deep breath and dived in. "Protec is big, I mean *really* big. And one of the reasons is a huge transfusion of megabucks at just the right time."

"Delaine's money."

"You got it. Conway gobbled up little companies like sharks swallow minnows at feeding time once he got his hands on her loot and her line of credit."

"Score one for our side. What about cash transactions in the last six months?"

"Protec tosses around millions like they came out of a

kid's Christmas account. But, oddly enough, that worked in our favor.''

"How so?"

"Because smaller amounts stick out like all hell. It goes like this. Protec-Europe is financed out of Zurich. If any funds are transferred from home—San Francisco or New York—to Zurich, it's always for a special reason. And it's always big bucks. About three weeks ago, there was a two-hundred-and-fifty-thousand-dollar transfer from New York to Zurich.''

"And that's small?"

"Smallest ever. It was earmarked for the Protec-Berlin slush fund.''

"Who controls that fund?''

"Lady by the name of Ursula Rhinemann.''

"Bingo,'' Carter whispered.

"What?"

"Nothing. Go ahead, where did the quarter mil go?''

"To buy a company château on the Havel River. But twenty-four hours after the down payment was made, it was withdrawn. There was a three-percent penalty, but that's peanuts.''

"Who did the money changing?''

"Deutschbank, here in Berlin. I've got a buddy over there who remembered the deal. The money wasn't transferred back into the Protec account. It was withdrawn in cash.''

"By Ursula Rhinemann?''

"You got it. But there's lots more. Personal on the wife. She drew two-hundred-and-fifty grand in cash from her personal account two days before she and Conway left for Europe.''

"The bastard doesn't get his fingers in at all, does he?'' Carter growled.

"Now come the last two twists.'' Erhanee paused there, savoring his beer and Carter's anticipation. "Oskar Hessling doesn't keep much cash in this country. In fact, he doesn't keep much cash, period. His horde is in gold, and he likes to buy it illegally. It's cheaper that way. He uses a guy named

Peter Rohenstaffer. A little over two weeks ago, Herr Peter made a two-hundred-and-fifty-thousand-dollar gold buy in London and ferried it to Zurich for Hessling. That news came from a speculator friend in London.''

"It all fits so far."

The grin on Erhanee's face spread from ear to ear. "Now comes the zinger. This morning, at the crack of opening, almost two hundred and fifty thousand in cash was deposited in the Protec slush fund at Deutschbank."

"By Ursula Rhinemann."

"You got it!"

Carter rubbed his chin in thought. "It's still circumstantial, but there's a definite trail. You got an address on this Rohenstaffer?"

"I thought you'd ask."

Erhanee passed across a slip of paper and dived into the food in front of him.

"Have a good lunch," Carter said, dropping some bills on the table. "I owe you one."

"It can't wait?"

"Not as fast as I think things are going to move in the next twenty-four hours," Carter said over his shoulder, and he headed for the foyer and a telephone.

According to Marty Jacobs, the AXE boys were tying the Voigts in knots, and the day was still young.

Horst Vintner was out, but Bruchner listened to the tale on Peter Rohenstaffer and agreed to pick Carter up in ten minutes.

He made one last call, to Lisa's suite at the Victoria.

"Dammit, Nick, I wish you'd check in more often," she said when she heard his voice.

"Been busy. What do you know about Ursula Rhinemann?"

"Name rings a bell, but I can't place it."

"I think she's the other woman in the triangle. I want you to call every mutual friend you and Delaine had, and see if your sister ever mentioned the name. Also, use your clout with Langley and have them dive into the records of international air carriers. I want to know the dates, if any, that Rhinemann visited the States.''

"Will do. By the way, I haven't exactly been idle.''

"Oh?"

"Delaine and I both bought a lot of our clothes at a little boutique off Fifth Avenue in New York called Figaro's. I know the owner well, and called her.''

"The red dress?''

"Yes. The saleswoman was named Kay. I talked to her, and she remembers the incident well. Delaine hated the dress and wouldn't even try it on. Stephan went into such a rage he frightened everyone in the shop. He finally won, and they bought the dress.''

They were both thinking the same thing; it was like ESP through the line.

*The dress was a beacon—better yet, an identifying target for the shooter.*

"It's thin, Lisa, but it might be another nail in the coffin.''

He hung up and hefted Erhanee's bulky bundle of computer printouts into the street. Bruchner was just pulling up to the curb.

"Here's the address.''

"What's that?'' The man nodded toward Carter's bundle.

"The financial life of Stephan Conway and Protec, my evening's reading. Have you got it?''

Bruchner passed across a thick, pulpy plastic envelope. "That stuff's pure gold on the street. The boys back there came along to make the arrest and make sure they get it back.''

Carter swiveled his head. Two plainclothes policemen followed them closely in an unmarked sedan. Their faces were square and grim, and their eyes never left the SSD car.

Carter put the one-pound bag of heroin in his inside coat pocket, and lit a cigarette. Herr Peter Rohenstaffer would be a small link, but at this point any link would do.

The address was in an old section of north Berlin, above Tegel Forest on Weiden Strasse. It dead-ended into a walk-through alley. Carter had Bruchner stop around the corner, and the two *cops* pulled in behind them.

Carter left the Protec report in the SSD car and moved down the block. Dusk had settled just enough to turn on the automatic streetlights.

Number 32 was indistinguishable from its other two-story neighbors. Carter rang the bell and put the hardest look he could muster on his face.

A pockmarked face under slicked-back gray hair appeared in a crack of the door. Carter wouldn't have known it was a woman if she hadn't spoken.

"What do you want?"

"I'd like to speak to Peter Rohenstaffer."

"What about?"

"I'd like to tell him myself."

"He isn't here."

"Where is he?"

"None of your business. He is out of town."

"I see. Who are you?"

"I am his mother."

"Oh, well, would you tell Herr Rohenstaffer that we have a mutual friend who has just died?"

"Who?"

"He'll know. Tell him I have to have an accounting."

The woman's mouth began to flap, but before any sound came out of it Carter turned and walked down the steps.

With the departure of daylight, a light mist had settled in, blurring the illumination from the streetlights into murky shadows.

Carter walked toward the corner where the two cars waited, then doubled back. Near the alley, he took up his watch beneath the stoop across the street and two houses closer to the alley than Number 32.

It was eight minutes by his watch when he saw the curtains of the front windows part slightly. Two minutes later the door of Number 32 opened, and a tall figure in a dark raincoat slipped down the steps. He carried a bulky briefcase, and from the speed of his movement and his carriage Carter put him somewhere in his mid-thirties.

He crossed the street, passed by the stoop where Carter waited, and headed toward the alley. Carter gave him five seconds and then followed. At the alley turn, the man was about ten yards ahead.

Carter caught up to him before the man heard his footsteps.

"You are Herr Peter Rohenstaffer?"

He turned to flee, but Carter tangled his own leg between the other man's and he went down. As he came up, the Killmaster grabbed his tie and put him against the wall.

"About three weeks ago you made a gold buy in London for Oskar Hessling . . ."

"Leave me alone! I don't know what you're talking about!"

"You ferried the gold to Zurich and deposited it for Hessling."

"Who are you?"

"A man who wants an answer . . . one answer."

"Go to hell."

He tried to bring a knee up into Carter's crotch. The Killmaster caught it on his hip and exploded his right fist into the man's gut.

"How did you find out Hessling was dead?"

This time he tried a foot to the shin. It connected, and Carter bit his lip in pain.

"Okay, mein Herr."

Carter dropped another in his belly, and tattooed his head against the brick wall.

"Stop! God, stop, you'll crack my skull . . .!"

Carter stopped, and flexed the muscle of his right forearm. Instantly he felt Hugo's smooth hilt in the palm of his hand. He put a half inch of the blade up Rohenstaffer's right nostril and gathered a handful of the man's hair to hold his head steady.

"I don't have time to play games, and I don't care if you live or die. Talk!"

"Tony called me . . . told me Oskar was dead." The man was close to sobbing.

"When were you supposed to pick up the second bundle?"

"Last night. Hessling was going to call me right after the

payoff was made. Tony called instead.''

"How much?''

"Same as the other, two hundred and fifty American.''

"Why would Tony call you?''

"He knows I'm Hessling's outside man.''

"So you know all Oskar's action?''

Silence.

Carter drew a little blood with Hugo.

"*Mein Gott*, don't kill me!''

"What's in the briefcase? Files? Records?''

"Yes.''

"Anything in there about the job that paid a half mil American?''

"No, that was a private deal. Hessling handled it all after the contact.''

"But you made the first contact?''

"Yes. It was a woman over the phone. She left ten thousand earnest money in a drop. I figured she was serious, so I put her onto Hessling.''

"What did she want for her money?''

"I don't know.'' Carter tickled the man's nose a little more. "I don't know, I swear!''

Carter pulled the blade from his nose but left it close. "After the deal was set, you must have made some of the arrangements. Hessling wouldn't get his hands dirty.''

"I don't know if I did or not. I do a lot of things for him.''

"Like steal a BMW motorcycle . . . or have it stolen.''

Rohenstaffer nodded.

"Where did you deliver it?''

"The airport parking lot. I left it with the keys and split.''

"What else?''

"Nothing.''

"There must be something else. You know that kind of fee calls for something big. Don't tell me you haven't guessed.''

The eyes went wild and started rolling. Carter knew he was losing him. This time Hugo's needle-sharp tip went to his neck.

"I didn't know until I heard it on the news!'' he sobbed. "I swear it! I figured it was going to be a hit, but I never guessed it would be the American!''

"You bargained for the gun, didn't you?''

"Yes. I only know him as the Turk. He sells out of a whorehouse in Wedding called the Nightbird Hotel.''

"I think you're telling me the truth.''

"I am, I swear.''

"What else?''

"Uh . . . uh, the car. I don't know whether it had anything to do with the hit or not, but I set up Gertrude Klammer to deliver a rented Mercedes to a garage on Wiebe Strasse.''

"You're a good man, Rohenstaffer.''

Carter dropped him with a slice to the back of the neck. He knelt and went to work on the briefcase with Hugo. It opened in seconds. Beneath a couple of shirts, some socks, and underwear, he found a gold mine.

He threw out the clothing and closed the briefcase. After stashing the heroin on Rohenstaffer, he jogged back down the block and slid into the SSD car beside Bruchner.

"Well?''

"Big business. He's sleeping peacefully back in the alley.''

"The junk on him?''

Carter nodded.

Bruchner climbed out of the car and walked back to the two policemen. He exchanged nods and words, and returned.

"They'll handle him. Damned dope peddlers. Anything else?''

"I'll tell you on the way. Do you know the Golden Calf on the Ku'Damm?''

"Who doesn't" Bruchner chuckled. He whirled the car into a U-turn and headed back toward the center of the city. "What's in the briefcase?''

"The life and times of Oskar Hessling. You can make copies for your people and the locals. The originals are bait for Hans-Otto Voigt.''

"What's at the Golden Calf, besides cheap snoops and whores?''

"A very nervous woman by the name of Gertrude Klammer.''

# ELEVEN

Bruchner backed him on the stairs while Carter knocked. There was no answer.

"Fräulein Klammer?"

The only sound was the chatter of the drinkers in the bar below and an occasional moan from one of the other rooms.

"I'm going to pick it."

Bruchner nodded.

Both the bartender and the man at the desk had told them that the woman was in her apartment and had been all day.

Carter's hands sweated as he used the two picks on the lock. He already had a pretty good idea of what he was going to find.

He wasn't wrong.

"Bruchner!"

"*Ja?*" Carter nodded him in and closed the door. "*Mein Gott.*"

There were two rooms: a living room and a tiny bedroom alcove behind tattered curtains.

Gertrude Klammer was arranged neatly on the bed, her eyes open, staring at the maze of cracks in the ceiling plaster. The angry red gash around her neck told the tale of her last seconds.

"Garrote?"

Carter nodded. "Piano wire, very fast and very quiet." Bruchner lifted the phone while Carter went to work on the

137

two rooms. He didn't expect to find much, but then he was only looking for one thing.

Whoever had done the number on Gertrude Klammer hadn't been interested in looking for anything. The place was as neat as a pin.

"They'll be here in fifteen minutes. I told them to use the back entrance and keep the excitement down."

"Good," Carter replied. He had just about finished, and had found nothing.

"You think it was the shooter, covering his tracks after he found out Hessling was dead?"

"Could be." Carter moved to the corpse.

*The things one gets used to doing*, he thought, gingerly pushing a finger into the fleshy part of the neck. The indentation stayed about three seconds. The woman had been dead about five hours.

The body was fully clothed, with no bruises or any other sign of a struggle.

Had Gertrude Klammer known her attacker? It would appear so.

Carefully Carter undid the buttons of her blouse, took a deep breath, and ran a finger under the right cup of her bra.

Nothing.

The other side was more productive: a thin, folded slip of paper. Carter glanced at it and handed it to Bruchner.

"The receipt for the Mercedes."

"Yeah," the Killmaster said. "That means I got the truth out of Herr Peter. Get on the phone and put a team out to find this Turk."

"Will do."

"Mind if I take your car back to the Victoria? I've got a lot of studying to do, and I want to get the Hessling papers copied."

"Go ahead," Bruchner said. "I'll wait here for the cleanup crew."

There was a drizzle in the air by the time Carter nosed the car up the Ku'Damm and around the Tiergarten toward the building housing the SSD offices.

Horst Vintner was still out of his office. Carter dropped off the briefcase, with instructions to have it delivered back to him at the Victoria the minute the contents had been copied, and then returned to the car.

"Any messages for Carter?" he asked when he returned to the hotel.

"*Ja, mein Herr.*"

Carter ripped the envelope. It was from Lisa.

"I'm at the Company offices. You ask a lot. Do you know how many flights have to be checked? If I get done by eight . . . dinner?"

Carter took the elevator to his floor. The instant he hit the room he sensed it: someone had paid a call. His extra pair of shoes were three inches off the mark at the foot of the bed. His suitcase had been moved slightly, just enough to detach the hair he had attached to one side of it with saliva.

Cautiously he went from corner to corner, wall to wall, phone to TV set.

Nothing.

Next he went through the bag and his personal effects—shirts, ties, socks, underwear—inspecting each item carefully before removing it.

In the bathroom he checked his shaving gear and smelled his aftershave and toothpaste. He even disassembled the stick deodorant. A tiny cyanide-tipped needle or pin stuck in the tube would work wonders.

He was almost satisfied that it had only been a search, when he noticed the slight crack between the porcelain and the rubber stopper on the toilet seat lid.

He got down on his hands and knees and used his penlight. There they were: two tiny springs set into the rubber stoppers.

Keeping his hands as steady as possible, he lifted the lid from the top of the reservoir tank. Two wires ran up, out of the flush pipe. They were attached to an oilskin bundle submerged in the water. Gently he replaced the lid and moved into the bedroom to the telephone.

"SSD," came a terse reply to the third ring.

"Horst Vintner, *bitte*."

The growling voice came on the line at once. "Vintner."

"Carter. How close are my copies to being done?"

"One moment." He was right back. "Another half hour. I've been checking them as they came off. Makes for very interesting reading."

"Good. When you have them delivered, have it done by a bomb expert."

"What?"

"Yeah, I've got about six sticks of dynamite in my toilet tank."

He hung up and dived for the Berlin directory.

"Der Bavarian."

"Erich Voigt, *bitte*."

"Herr Voigt has not come in."

"Yeah? Well, you tell him Carter called. The bomb didn't go boom."

"What is this . . .?"

"This is bullshit. Tell him I'm doubling the pressure."

Carter hung up and returned to the bathroom. Gingerly he splashed water on his face and then sat down to read the rise to power of Stephan Conway.

Oncoming dusk and the onset of a light but warm drizzle had driven most of the bathers from the grassy banks of the Hallensee. Those that were left kept to their nude hedonism.

The Turk lay on the grass directly below the concession stand. About fifty yards out in the lake, a raft bobbed at its moorings. Unlike the couples around him, the Turk wore a suit.

He was where he was supposed to be. Where was the woman?

He had checked her source out with Hamburg. She was legit. She had agreed to the price over the phone. Not so unusual. People who wanted guns in a hurry usually didn't quibble about price.

Near the Turk's hip, wound tightly in a waterproof bag attached to a belt, was a sample of the merchandise, a silenced Walther PPK.

She had told him on the phone that she wanted ten of them. The Turk had jacked the price up a thousand marks per unit.

She had agreed, as long as the quality was good. She had also hinted that there might be a larger order to follow.

He checked the fading light. It must be close to six o'clock. She was almost a half hour late.

And then he saw her. She was directly in front of him, standing near the water. She looked like some kind of raven-haired goddess, with the upper half of her body silhouetted against the gray sky. Her clothing was a halter bra and a wraparound skirt.

*I will be wearing a matching black and white striped top and skirt.*

Then her hands started working, and the skirt fell to the grass.

She stood, making sure that the Turk had spotted her, then she turned toward the water and stretched to her toes.

The Turk's mouth watered. Maybe he could extract a little extra payment. She was beautiful, not the kind of woman with whom the Turk normally came in contact.

The long legs seemed to quiver with strength clear up to the equally quivering, well-rounded buttocks. Her stomach was flat, indented between sharp hip bones. The breasts were large, firmly jutting from her rib cage.

"Maybe I give you a deal on price after all, woman," the Turk muttered, moving the belt around his middle and fastening it.

She arched her body into the water, and the Turk went in after her. The sun had beat down most of the day, until about an hour before, making the water warm.

She crawled up onto the raft with lithe ease, and stretched out with her toes facing the grassy slope and her head toward the center of the lake. The Turk joined her in the same position, his thigh nudging hers.

"You brought the sample?"

Her German was accented slightly, but the Turk couldn't place her native tongue.

"I did."

"Let me see."

He removed the belt and pushed the pouch in front of their

heads so it couldn't be seen by anyone on the bank. He unzipped it, peeled back the inner, waterproof lining, and extracted the Walther.

"The silencer?"

He removed the silencer and screwed it into the snout of the Walther. "It is a prime piece, completely rebuilt. I can get you all you want."

She had rolled to her left side and molded her body to his. It was difficult, with her soft breasts caressing his shoulder, for the Turk to keep his mind on business.

She fumbled in the darkness beneath her breasts and removed a small oilskin pouch. Each movement made more sweat break out on the Turk's body.

"I have to say, this is the strangest way I have ever made a delivery."

She chuckled. "But you must admit it is private. No one on shore is paying any attention to us, and no one can hear us."

"True."

She handed him three shells from the pouch. "Load it."

"Load it . . .?"

"Of course. I don't want merchandise with faulty firing pins."

The Turk shrugged against her, and ejected the clip. He inserted the three shells. He jammed the clip back into the butt and armed it. "Okay?"

"Yes." She nodded, rolling her body partially over his. "Fire, once, into the water."

He shifted the gun to his right hand and fired. Her hand was just above his, her warm breath on the back of his neck. Her bra must have slipped down. He could feel her bare nipples hardening against his back.

"Satisfied?" he stammered.

"Again." He fired a second shell into the water. "Now let me."

She reached for the gun. Her whole body moved over him. The feel of her skin was intoxicating, so intoxicating that he failed to notice that on her right hand she wore a glove, a clear plastic surgeon's glove.

She lifted the gun from his hand, but instead of firing the third and final round into the water, she turned the barrel toward his head. Before he could stop her, the blunt nose of the silencer was grinding into the soft hollow behind his right ear.

"What the . . .?"

"Shhh, be very still and very quiet."

"What are you doing?"

"I'm angling the barrel so if I fire, the bullet will go directly into your brain."

"You crazy bitch . . .!"

He froze. Her left hand had moved around to place a piece of paper and a small pen on the raft under his face.

"Read that and sign it."

The Turk had to wipe the sweat with nervous fingers from his eyes before they would focus.

"You are a crazy bitch!"

"Didn't you supply the F1 for Hessling?"

Silence. She ground the silencer deeper.

"Oow, damn you!"

"Didn't you?"

"I've got a lawyer! You pigs can't get away with—"

She chuckled in his ear. "I am not SSD or the police."

"Then why . . .?"

"Blackmail. I know who hired Hessling to find Klaus-witz."

"I don't know Klauswitz."

"No matter. When it all goes together, there will be a great deal of money. The evidence must be overwhelming. If you cooperate, you will get this confession back. You might even make some of the profit."

She could feel his body relax slightly beneath hers.

"But if the police get this . . ." he stammered.

"They won't. Sign!"

The Turk took the pen in his shaking right hand. He closed his left hand over his right wrist to keep it steady, and scrawled his signature across the bottom of the page: Demetrius Baclevic.

"Very good."

She pulled the pen and paper from beneath his face and fired the third slug into his brain.

She folded the paper carefully and returned it and the pen to the pouch. When the pouch was anchored securely in her bra, Anna Palmitkov slid into the water and swam back to the grassy shoreline.

It was just after seven o'clock. With any luck, she would have a meeting arranged between herself and Stephan Conway before the evening was out.

Lisa called at seven. Carter broke long enough to pad down the hall to her suite for food.

The atmosphere was tense as he brought her up to date on what he had learned.

Ursula Rhinemann had made at least two trips a month to the States in the last six months, some to New York, some to San Francisco. It could be all business, or there could have been a lot of hanky-panky mixed in. There was no way of telling without checking all of Stephan Conway's movements in the States as well, and that would be very difficult.

Lisa would start on it in the morning.

"It's all loose, isn't it?" she sighed. "Circumstantial."

"So far," Carter admitted. "If Rhinemann is part of the triangle, it looks as though Conway has put her up front with everything. If there is a fall, it's her word against his."

They finished the meal in silence. Carter didn't tell her that a little over an hour before, the bomb boys had removed eight sticks of dynamite from the toilet in his room.

From the haggard look on her face, she couldn't take that knowledge along with everything else she had absorbed during the last few days.

At the door she kissed him perfunctorily on the cheek. It was pretty obvious to Carter that she wanted—and needed—to be alone as much as he.

"Get a good night's sleep," he murmured, squeezing her shoulder gently.

"I'll try."

"Take a pill."

Again in his room, he dived back into the Hessling papers.

They said a lot, but nothing that would do him any good nailing Conway. The only real information was that, by reading between the lines, Herr Hessling did have some strong contacts in the Eastern sector that were very profitable.

Carter was almost finished, when there was a light tap at the door.

"Yeah?"

"Vintner."

Carter opened the door and the big man marched into the room. He dropped into an easy chair, loosened his tie, and undid his top shirt buttons.

"Long day?"

"You know it. Your boys have started World War Three out there. Thank God the Voigts don't know where to hit back!"

"Other than blowing up my ass . . . literally," Carter growled. "Drink? I've got brandy and scotch."

"Brandy's fine. Any results?"

"Not yet." Carter handed him the glass. It was gone in one swallow. "Anything on the Turk?"

"His name is Demetrius Baclevic. And he's disappeared."

"Tipped?"

"Who knows? Maybe old man Voigt will tell you, if you ever get to him."

Carter brought the SSD man up to date on every piece of info he had garnered that day. Vintner sat, slouched, scowling at the empty glass rolling between his big hands.

"So, what have we got?" he said at last. "We've got a lot of little things that point to Ursula Rhinemann, and from her we guess Conway."

"But nothing that would nail him," Carter added.

"How's the sister taking it?"

"Rough."

"How do you figure it?"

Carter sighed, finished his drink, and refilled both their glasses.

"Conway marries Delaine for her money and contacts.

The money works, the marriage doesn't. It gets worse when Rhinemann comes on the scene. Somebody tries to blackmail Conway. He sees it as a way to threaten his own life. So he sends Rhinemann out to hunt for a shooter.''

"And she finds Hessling."

"Right. The irony is that Hessling probably found *her*, only she didn't know it."

Carter decided to come clean about the Peter Limpton/ Boris Simonov connection with Hessling.

"My guess is Hessling hired the shooter, and gave him instructions to waste Delaine and do everything he could to make it look like Conway was the target. Hessling keeps all the marbles, and when everything cools down, he's *really* got some blackmail ammunition.''

Vintner pulled himself from the chair. "It would fit. But with Hessling dead, so is the proof.''

"Unless we get the shooter.''

"Yeah, unless we get the shooter.''

"Check in with me in the morning.''

"Will do,'' the chief inspector grunted, and closed the door behind him.

Carter sat in an easy chair by the window, turned off the lamp, and stared out at the city.

Was the shooter still out there, or was he long gone? Hessling's phone call to Limpton/Simonov would indicate that the man was sure he was going to get the goods. That would mean that Hessling had the shooter on ice in case he needed him to back up the blackmail shot.

Thinking about it made Carter weary. He dozed. And the doze deepened and became sleep.

The phone brought him upright in the chair. He snapped on the light and glanced at his watch. It was three in the morning.

"Carter here.''

"All right, you son of a bitch, call off your dogs!''

"Nice of you to call, Erich.''

"My limo will be at the side door of the hotel in fifteen minutes.''

"And Hans-Otto?''

"My father is on the island waiting for you."

"Nice to do business with you, Erich."

He cut the connection and redialed AXE Berlin. When he got Marty Jacobs on the line, he gave the order to halt the war.

Then he took a long shower, shaved, and climbed into clean clothes.

Forty-five minutes after Erich Voigt's phone call, he went downstairs.

*Screw' em*, the Killmaster thought. *They made me wait two days, they can wait an extra half hour.*

# TWELVE

The estate was exactly what the term implied and then some. It covered a good-size island in the middle of the Havel River.

They covered him from both sides as they got out of the Mercedes limo. At the dock they patted him down and found Wilhelmina. One of them started to stick his hairy paw under Carter's jacket, and the Killmaster grabbed his wrist.

"Oh, no, you don't," he hissed. "This Christian doesn't meet the lions naked."

"Iss impossible!"

"Then we end the cease-fire."

"Wait here."

He stomped down to the waiting launch and started working a phone. Carter turned to the other one.

"Got a match?"

Reluctantly a lighter flared, and Carter inhaled deeply. The cigarette was half gone when the angry goon returned, angrier than ever.

"Come!"

It was a fifteen-minute ride, and another five-minute walk up from the boathouse. Hans-Otto didn't slack on security. During the walk, Carter counted nine men armed with machine pistols or shotguns. Loping at each man's side was a big German shepherd.

The Sixth Panzer Division would have had a hard time cracking this one, Carter thought.

As he walked between the two men through heavily forested formal gardens, the Killmaster ticked off what he had gleaned from police files about Hans-Otto Voigt.

He had been actively anti-Nazi during World War II. In his twenties he had joined a small elite group in Berlin devoted to overthrowing the Nazis by internal espionage.

Right after the war, he survived by using the same smuggling avenues to form a huge black market. But as well as being a survivor, Voigt was a born leader, cunning and ruthless.

It was only a matter of time before smuggling and the black market were just a small part of his operations. By the late fifties, Voigt was the acknowledged kingpin of crime in West Berlin and northern Germany. And since then he had been able to keep that empire intact.

The villa was built on a rise directly in the center of the island. The walkway up from the water was a long, winding affair that passed outlying houses, gardens, and several more gun-toting guards.

Architecturally, it was a mishmash of Rhine River castle and mock English Tudor. It appeared to have been built by some long-dead or crazed Teutonic knight rather than by a modern, living gangland overlord.

One of two huge, brass-studded oak doors opened, and Carter stepped into a massive hallway. Erich Voigt awaited him.

"I want your gun."

"The only way you'll get it is to take it."

The younger man stepped forward. Carter didn't move. He smiled.

"You bastard."

"I didn't come to listen to you whine, Erich."

"My father is in the hothouse. This way."

Carter followed him through a maze of corridors, glancing into well-furnished rooms as they moved. There were fresh-cut flowers everywhere.

From the outside, the house had loomed large. Inside it was enormous. Even though it was comparatively new, it had a sprawling, solid aura of aged splendor; Carter credited it to good taste in construction and the dominant use of expensive woods and stone for building materials.

Erich led him through wide, open French doors into a tiny Eden, completely surrounded by a high, immaculately clipped myrtle hedge. The hedge surrounded a sea of camellias, . oleander, carnations, and myriad botanical marvels Carter couldn't name.

Above and around the whole was glass, keeping out the river breezes, the city smells, and keeping the interior what it was . . . a hothouse.

In the middle of the sea of flowers sat an ornate fountain. Beside the fountain was a table and four chairs. One of the chairs was occupied by a short, wide man. The face was grizzled with age but still handsome in the chiseled Teutonic mold. The eyes were piercingly blue under heavy dark brows that didn't match the mane of steel-gray hair.

"Are you Carter?" The voice was growlingly husky, as if he had polished off a carton of cigarettes within the last hour.

"I'm Carter."

"A few years ago I would have just had you shot and buried in the Havel."

"A few years ago I would have dealt directly with you and would not have had to deal with the boy."

At the word *boy*, Erich came forward with his fists clenched.

"Erich, sit down," the old man hissed. "He's right."

Erich sat. So did Carter. Hans-Otto leaned forward, a glint of impishness in his hard blue eyes. "You like my garden?"

"Lovely. The flowers are beautiful."

"Good. If you die tonight, I will see you get the finest bouquet. Why do you cost me so much money?"

"Because I wanted to trade with you, and your son has stone ears."

"So. What do you have? What do you want?"

Carter hefted the briefcase to the table and opened it. "I have Oskar Hessling."

The old man rifled through the papers quickly, but Carter could tell that he didn't miss a thing. When he was through,

he slapped the case closed and, in the same movement,
backhanded Erich across the face.

"*Dummkopf!*"

"Papa . . ."

"Shut up! Get out of my sight!" When the younger Voigt
was gone, Hans-Otto turned his gaze back to Carter as he
tapped the case. "Who are you?"

"Somebody important."

"You must be, the way you turn my people upside down.
This"—he tapped the case harder—"this, I would kill for.
Who do you want killed?"

"Herr Voigt"—Carter slowly lit a cigarette, speaking in a
low, modulated tone—"if I want someone killed, I'll do it
myself."

Voigt's hard blue eyes squinted, then he nodded. "*Ja*, I
believe you would."

"I want information, and a body . . . live, if possible. I
want to know who hired him, and who the shooter is who
tried for the American, Stephan Conway."

"I didn't hire him."

"I wouldn't be here if I thought you had. When you find
out who the shooter is, I want your help locating and getting
him."

"Agreed. What else?"

"I don't know yet. Maybe something . . . maybe
nothing."

Hans-Otto was a man of quick decisions. The old eyes
blinked once and the big head came up with a jerk. "Erich!"

"Yes?"

"Get me a telephone out here, and some beer. What kind
of beer do you want, Carter?"

"Dutch, it costs more."

"Dutch beer! And move!"

Carter heard the younger man sprint into the house, and he
leaned back in his chair. His hunch was right. If anyone could
find out who and where the shooter was, it was Hans-Otto
Voigt.

● ● ●

Anna Palmitkov rapped on the door. It was opened at once, but only a crack. No light was lit and the face in the crack was in shadows.

"Yes?"

"Fräulein Rhinemann?"

"Yes."

"I just talked to you on the phone."

"Come in, hurry!"

Anna Palmitkov darted through the door. It was quickly closed and locked behind her. As soon as the lights were turned on, she walked down into the sunken living room and turned to face the other woman with a flourish.

"Who are you?" Ursula asked, clutching a half-empty glass of whiskey between her two trembling hands.

"Who I am is of no consequence. I assure you, I have the material I mentioned so vaguely on the telephone."

Anna slipped the big bag she carried from her shoulder. She rummaged in it and withdrew three sheets of paper and a manila folder.

"Sit down," she said curtly, glancing up at the other woman.

Ursula flushed. "This is my flat. How dare you—"

The Russian woman's hand arced like a whip and struck like a darting snake. The flat palm cracked against the side of Ursula's head, sending her sprawling and the glass of whiskey crashing against the mantel.

"Now will you listen?" she hissed.

"Yes." Tears were streaming down Ursula Rhinemann's beautiful face. Her body shook, and she was sure she wouldn't be able to hold down what little food she had in her stomach. "What do you want?"

"Nothing, I assure you, that you will not be able to give. Now, I am going to tell you a story . . ."

For the next hour, Ursula listened. The more she listened, the whiter and sicker she became.

*She knew! This woman knew practically the whole thing, almost down to the time when she and Stephan had first conceived the plan!*

"This is the confession of a woman named Gertrude Klammer. Small, by itself, but a link. Another, stranger, link is this statement by a minor illegal arms dealer, Demetrius Baclevic."

"I know none of these people . . ."

"Read!"

Ursula read, dropped the papers, and ran from the room. The sounds of vomiting from the adjoining bath didn't bother Anna Palmitkov. She fixed a drink from the other woman's well-stocked sideboard and lit a cigarette.

Eventually Ursula returned, shaken, and resumed her seat. "I know nothing of this."

"Don't you?" The third sheet of paper was pressed into Ursula's hand. "This is the statement of Dieter Klauswitz, to the effect that he was hired by Oskar Hessling to assassinate Delaine Berrington Conway. It also states that you and Stephan Conway ordered, through Oskar Hessling, this murder."

"That's impossible! The killer didn't even know that Stephan and I—"

Ursula suddenly screamed and clamped her lips tightly shut.

Anna Palmitkov's smile was that of a predator.

"We have Dieter Klauswitz in an East German prison at this very moment."

"It means nothing!" Ursula gasped. "It means absolutely nothing! None of this can be connected to myself or Stephan!"

"Perhaps not, directly. But several weeks ago one of our agents was working with Oskar Hessling. His cover name was Peter Limpton. His real name is Boris Simonov. He turned out to be a traitor after he was caught by the Americans, but several of the operations he initiated bore fruit even without his knowledge. These, for instance."

From the manila envelope, Anna produced ten eight-by-ten prints. All were in living, fleshy color. Each of them was from a different angle, and they all showed Ursula Rhinemann and Stephan Conway in various stages of making love.

Ursula bent her face into her hands. Silent tears dripped from her fingers and all the starch went out of her body.

"You're not the police," she said finally, looking up, her voice flat and devoid of emotion. "What do you want?"

A smile of victory creased Anna Palmitkov's face. "That's more like it," she said, producing another sheet of paper and moving toward the other woman. "Here is an updated list of the equipment Oskar Hessling has already tried to blackmail Stephan Conway for. There are also detailed instructions as to where and how they should be routed."

"Stephan will never agree!"

"I think he will," Anna said, calmly sipping her drink. "I think your lover will agree to anything to save his skin. Call him."

"Now?"

"Now. I'm sure he has a private phone."

"Yes." Ursula nodded dumbly. "He installs a scrambler line wherever he goes . . . for business."

"Good, even better. Call him!"

Still weeping, Ursula tugged the phone toward her and dialed.

"Yes?"

"Stephan . . . it's me."

"Ursula, how dare you call me here . . . even on this phone!"

"Stephan, something very important has come up—"

"Dammit, Ursula, can't it wait until morning?"

"No, dammit, it can't!"

"All right, all right, darling . . . calm down. What is it?"

In a halting, weepy voice, Ursula read the three confessions, and then told him about the pictures.

When she finished, there was a long, deathly silence on the other end of the line.

"Stephan? . . . Are you still there?"

"Yes, I'm here. I'm thinking. Is the woman still there?"

"Yes."

"Put her on!"

She held the receiver out to the Russian. "He wants to talk to you."

Anna Palmitkov removed a Cartier earring and spoke into the phone. "Yes."

"Who are you?"

"It doesn't matter. What does matter is that I am willing to suppress the information I have in return for certain . . . indulgences on your part."

"You're asking me to commit treason!"

"Murder, treason . . . it's all the same."

"Damn you!"

"I have very little time, Mr. Conway. What do you say?"

"I'd like to tell you to kiss my ass."

"I'm sure you would." She chuckled mirthlessly.

"I'll have to see you first . . . talk to you in person."

Anna paused, reasoned. "That could be arranged."

"I'm due to inspect my Spandau plant in the morning. There is a beer hall on Pininberger Strasse in Staaken, near the wall."

"I can find it."

"Shall we say noon?"

"Noon would be fine. *Guten Morgen, Herr Conway.*"

Anna hung up the phone and replaced her earring.

"He's not going to do it," Ursula said, her already wide eyes even wider.

"He wants to talk. But I'm sure, my dear, that he will do it."


"Are you awake?" she asked from the darkness beside him.

"Yes."

Carter moved his arm over her stomach, but there was no response. She had been waiting in his room, in fact in his bed, when he returned from the meeting with Voigt.

"What happened?" she had asked.

Carter told her as he undressed and slid into the bed beside her.

They talked, and the more they hashed it over, the more desultory she had become. Carter made overtures and she responded, weakly. The lovemaking was mechanical, no passion, minimal result.

Afterward, they had lain for many moments in silence, apart.

Now it seemed she wanted more talk, and Carter wasn't really up to it.

"I've got a gut feeling, right there"—she pressed his arm—"that no matter what you uncover, it will all lead to the Rhinemann woman, and Stephan will end up walking away."

"Not if I can help it."

"Perhaps not even you, Nick, can work a miracle this time. The more we learn about Stephan, the more I realize that he is rich, clever, powerful, and completely amoral. People like that can get away with anything. There are no laws for them."

The dull monotone of her voice struck him. It wasn't like her, and the fatalistic viewpoint she was taking could be dangerous.

"Hey," he said, squeezing her.

"What?"

"I think you've got post-coital depression."

"Don't patronize me, Nick."

"All right," he sighed, "I won't. We need the shooter. I think Hans-Otto will give him to us."

"And then, hopefully, everything will fall into place?"

"Hopefully. Everything in this business is bits and pieces. You only pray they come together."

"Remember Hong Kong?" she asked, her voice raspy with mood.

"Yeah."

"You stayed with me all that night and the next day. That next night I woke up and gave you a name. You left my hospital room. I know where you went and what you did, Nick."

Gently, Carter rolled away from her.

He remembered. He had very carefully worked the Chinese underworld and gotten himself an Uzi. Then he had gone to a Kowloon warehouse and blown away three men.

No report had ever been filed, nor was any connection ever made.

But Lisa had known.

Suddenly he was conscious that she was up, out of the bed, and slipping into her robe.

"Where . . .?"

"You need your sleep," she replied, moving toward the door. "Tomorrow is a big day . . . for both of us."

He started to object, but the door was already closing behind her.

Carter was bone-tired, but he lay awake for a long time after she left, worrying about the way he thought her mind was perhaps playing tricks on her.

It was first light when at last he allowed his eyes to close and let sleep overtake him.

# THIRTEEN

Stephan Conway slid the photos and the sheets of paper back into the manila envelope and dropped them on a table between himself and the woman. Even though they were in a very private, screened cubicle, he looked around before speaking, as if someone were peering over his shoulder.

"Other than the photographs, it's pure supposition," he growled. "And so what? Many married men have affairs. Half the men working for me are probably screwing their secretaries."

"If they are working for you," the dark-haired woman replied coolly, "they probably are."

"You are a snide bitch."

Her red lips played with a smile. "Your opinions don't bother me, nor do they interest me. Added to what you have seen, we can send Klauswitz back to the West in person to tell his story."

"It still wouldn't touch me."

"Perhaps not. But it would put a rather large dent in your credibility. You could, as you Americans put it, kiss politics good-bye."

Stephan Conway rubbed his temples. "What do you want?"

Anna Palmitkov passed across the same list she had presented to Ursula Rhinemann in the wee hours of that morning. Conway perused it, then slammed it on the table in disgust.

"It's treason!"

"It's business. And if you don't want to do business . . ."

She gathered the list and the manila folder and started to rise.

"Sit down." Conway sighed and mashed his unlit cigar into a coffee cup. "If I agree, I want more in return than this material."

"Such as . . .?"

"All traces eradicated."

Anna Palmitkov lit a cigarette. She inhaled deeply and let the smoke seep from her nostrils. "The man who supplied the rifle is already dead. So is the woman, Fräulein Klammer."

The Russian agent fully expected the man across from her to blanch, gasp, or otherwise show some shock at the realization of her ruthlessness.

She was totally unprepared for his own ruthlessness.

"Good. I want this Dieter Klauswitz dead as well. I want his body delivered to the West German SSD, along with another confession that it was me he was planning to kill."

"I think that can be arranged."

"It *will* be arranged," Conway hissed. "And that's not all. I want Ursula out of the way, and I want it to appear to be an accident."

It was the woman's turn to blink. She had been trained to forswear any emotion, to kill without question, to use her body for any reason under orders. There was literally nothing she would not do to further her cause.

Yet even she was shocked.

"That may be difficult."

"But it can be done," he countered.

"Yes, it can be done."

"I'm leaving early this afternoon for Munich. I want to be there, out of Berlin, when it happens."

"Excuse me. I must make a phone call."

Stephan Conway ordered fresh coffee and a brandy while he waited. He unwrapped a fresh cigar, and this time lit it. It was going well by the time the Russian returned.

"Well?"

"Call her. Tell her you must see her in person, but not in West Berlin. Tell her to drive through East Germany and enter the West on the Number Fifteen autobahn toward Hamburg. Tell her to leave at six this evening. Do you have that so far?"

"Of course."

"At Ludwigslust, she is to take the highway north toward Schwerin. Tell her that you will intercept her on that road. That is why her timing must be precise."

"It will look like an accident."

"It will."

Conway nodded. He even smiled. "She drives—"

"—a new 190 SL gray Mercedes convertible, license number D944-941. We are very thorough, Mr. Conway. Now, your part of the bargain."

Conway checked his watch. "I can have the order to our research facility in California within the hour. They will transfer it to our warehouse in Pennsylvania. It can be on the five o'clock flight from Dulles, Washington time."

"That means it will be here at five in the morning."

"Barring weather in Frankfurt."

"At noon tomorrow, Mr. Conway, the West German authorities will be informed to pick up the body of Dieter Klauswitz at Checkpoint Charlie."

"And the originals . . . the confessions and the photos?"

"Will be delivered to you in Munich as soon as the equipment is in East Berlin. I, myself, will escort the transfer."

"And if you get caught out of Frankfurt?"

"There will be someone to take my place. We will just have to try another shipment, won't we?"

This took Conway slightly by surprise, but he quickly recovered and countered by going right back on the offensive.

"I don't know who you are, but I can guess what you are: Russian, and probably KGB. Well, you know what? I don't give a rat's ass as long as I get mine. I have as much money, as much power, and as many contacts as most Third World countries."

"I am sure you do."

"Remember it. Because, when this is over, if you ever try and contact me again, I'll have you killed just like I did my wife. Only it won't be so quick and painless. And I'll do it no matter where you are, even in Moscow."

With that, he was gone.

Anna Palmitkov followed a trail of smoke down the cigarette in her hand.

The fingers holding it were shaking.

"Herr Carter?"

"*Ja.*" Carter recognized the voice on the phone at once, and he rolled from the bed, shaking the fog from his brain.

"Need I say who this is?"

"No. What have you got?"

"Our man was hired through Oskar Hessling. It was done by a woman who made the original contact in the U.S. But somehow I feel you already had that information, correct?"

"Yes. I was testing you."

"I respect that. The man you want was very difficult to identify since he was not a pro."

"He wasn't?"

"No, but he was extremely qualified. Part of that bastard Hessling's genius was finding people like this."

"Who is he?"

"His name is Dieter Klauswitz."

Carter lit a cigarette and let the smoke burn his lungs as he listened to a brief history of the shooter.

"Where can I get him?" he said at last.

"I am afraid that will be difficult. Right now, Klauswitz is being held in an East German prison. He is also being closely guarded as a prisoner of the state."

"Damn."

"That is all I can tell you, Herr Carter. You mentioned you might have need of another service before our agreement was complete?"

"No . . . wait, maybe. Hold on!"

Carter dropped the phone. He padded to the bathroom and ran the sink full of cold water. Quickly he doused his head twice into the water to clear the cobwebs.

*Risky*, he thought, his brain functioning on all cylinders again, *but it might provide the leverage*.

"Voigt?"

"I am still here."

"I want you to kidnap a woman and hold her."

"That will take some time, surveillance, a setup . . ."

"I want it done sometime tonight."

"I will arrange it."

"The name is Ursula Rhinemann . . ."

"Ursula?"

"Yes."

"Go to the corner phone and call me."

Conway replaced the receiver on its cradle and snapped his two bulky suitcases shut. He always did his own packing. It was a fetish of his, knowing where everything was at all times, even his underwear and handkerchiefs.

He grabbed the phone on the first ring.

"It's me, what happened?"

"Listen, darling, I don't have time to tell you everything now. I must see you."

"But how? It would be too dangerous for us to be seen—"

"I don't care, Ursula, darling. I have to see you, now most of all."

"I suppose it could be just business," she said after thinking for a moment. "Should I come to the hotel?"

"No . . . no, I want you to drive into West Germany."

"What?"

Carefully, Conway gave her the instructions the Russian woman had given him. And then he repeated them.

"But where do I meet you?"

"Just keep driving. I will intercept you."

Sobs came over the phone. "Oh, Stephan, it's all going to catch up with us, isn't it!"

"No, no, it isn't, not if we keep our heads. Just do as I say, Ursula, and we'll be together forever . . . soon. And, Ursula . . .?"

"Yes?"

"Don't tell a soul where you are going."

"I won't. Does that woman who came last night have anything to do with this?"

Conway almost replied in the negative but thought better of it. "Yes, in a way."

"Oh, Stephan, you're not going to give them the equipment, are you?"

"Ursula, how can you even think it? What we have done is for us, but I would never become a traitor. You know that."

"Yes, of course I do. I love you, Stephan."

"And I love you, darling. I'll see you tonight." He hung up and brusquely moved to the door. "John? . . . John, where the devil are you?"

"Right here, sir."

"Is the car ready?"

"Yes, sir, and the plane is ready to leave at Tegel."

"Good. Get my bags. Let's get the hell out of here!"

Carter dialed Lisa's suite, and a voice still full of sleep answered.

"It's me," he said. "Feel better?"

"Not much. Just sleepy."

"Go ahead, get lots. If we can wrap this thing up by tonight, we head for Munich."

"Munich?"

"To put the vise to Stephan Conway. He's gone down there early; I just talked to Vintner. I'm headed for his office now."

"Anything new?"

"We know who the shooter is."

"Nick, I'm coming along."

"No need. Sit tight, I'll keep you informed."

He hung up before she could ask more questions, and headed for the elevator. The SSD car and driver Vintner had assigned him were waiting at the curb.

The ride was twenty minutes through the drizzle and rain-slick streets.

"Good morning," Carter said, pouring himself a hot mug of coffee and taking a seat across from the SSD man.

"It's afternoon. Here's the Klauswitz file. He's got a short rap sheet, but the background fits the profile."

"Any chance of bargaining for him?"

"Depends if they know what they've got."

Carter nodded and sipped the steaming brew as he leafed through the file. "That's what I was thinking. Also, if he went over right after the hit, it wasn't Klauswitz who snuffed Klammer."

"After reading that, I think you'll agree it wouldn't be his style anyway. He might take her with his bare hands, but never a piece of piano wire. I've sent feelers over the wall. We'll just have to wait. *Ja*, Bruchner, what is it?"

Carter looked up. Bruchner was in the doorway, a mixture of disgust and puzzlement clouding his features.

"The Turk. They found him on a raft in the middle of the Hallensee about an hour ago . . . dead."

"How did he get it?" Carter asked.

"Gunshot, one slug behind the right ear. They already identified the gun. It's one of a whole case stolen about a month ago from the military barracks armory at Protag."

"On a raft?" Vintner said.

"Yes, sir. His prints are the only ones on the gun. They're calling it a suicide."

Carter and Vintner exchanged looks. Their eyes said it all: bullshit.


The bad weather had gotten worse. Through the tall windows the sky above West Berlin had turned to the color of lead with the fading light. The drizzle drifted across the city in a gray wash that made Carter even more depressed than he already felt.

It wasn't difficult to put together now. The KGB or the East German Stasis—or both—had nailed Dieter Klauswitz. Not only had they nailed him, but they were also already moving on what he had told them.

A fast phone call to D.C. and some rapid-fire questions to Limpton/Simonov had filled in a few of the gaps. There were things under the intensive questioning that he had remembered telling Anna Palmitkov. Such as the connection he had set up with Oskar Hessling to blackmail Stephan Conway.

When Dieter Klauswitz fell in their lap, it was like manna from heaven, or fruits of a good operation, depending on how one looked at it.

Taking the Klammer killing and the Turk "suicide" together fit for Carter. Chances were that an East German team had been sent over to do the kills. That meant the East had already figured it out and was way ahead of the West.

Next step?

Get what they wanted out of Conway.

*God knows*, Carter thought, if he were guessing right, *they have more than enough ammunition*.

They had someone set to watch Conway and his entourage in Munich. In Berlin it had been difficult to keep tabs on his every move. Vintner had snidely informed Carter that "Herr Conway has a great deal of very influential friends. The two men I had on him were pulled after a few phone calls to Bonn."

Politics, Carter thought, looking at the chiaroscuro of auto and city lights far below.

"Damn."

Carter whirled around. Jamil Erhanee sat at a huge horseshoe desk in front of a bank of computer screens. He leaned far back in his chair, his thumbs digging into his eyes.

"You need some more coffee, Jamil?"

"No, I need forty fingers and two brains. Can't you get this stuff legit? Flash a badge or something?"

Carter chuckled. "Conway covers his ass too well for that, I'm afraid. Keep at it."

Carter moved to a table laden with sandwiches and a huge coffee maker.

"Getting into his bank accounts was a piece of cake compared to this," the Indian groaned. "Christ, Nick, shipping, inventory, and classification on the output of a company like Protec is like trying to crack Fort Knox with a water cannon!"

Carter handed him a fresh cup of steaming coffee. "Keep at it, my friend. If the KGB has a lever on Conway, I want to know if he bends or topples. Right now it's all we've got.''

With a sigh, Erhanee sipped his coffee and rolled forward in his chair to tap out more sequences in an effort to find the key that would let him into the Protec computers.

The phone rang. Carter noted the line and grabbed it. ''Carter here.''

''It's Lisa, Nick. Vintner gave me this number. What's new?''

''Not much.'' Quickly he brought her up to date.

''They've got him,'' she replied, ''and they'll turn him. He'll do anything to escape something like this and keep himself lily white!''

Again there was that tremor in her voice bordering on hysteria.

''Calm down, Lisa, we're doing all we can.''

''I know, I know. It's just . . . well, dammit, it's frustrating!''

''I know it is . . . damned frustrating.''

''Anything I can do?''

''No. Stay cool at the hotel. I'll call you if anything breaks.''

''Thanks. 'Night.''

''Yeah.''

Carter dropped the phone and checked his watch.

It was seven o'clock. Hans-Otto's boys would just be moving in on Ursula Rhinemann.


Ursula cleared the last barricade and made the powerful engine whine as she shifted through the gears. Ahead, the autobahn twisted like a white ribbon.

In the rearview mirror, she could see that the black Volvo was still following her. The car had picked her up at the Spandau Gate and stayed with her, matching her speed, all through East Germany.

She had slowed several times to a crawl. Always the Volvo slowed with her. Halfway across the GDR, she had decided that Stephan was in the Volvo. Who else would follow her in such a manner?

She resumed a normal speed for the autobahn, which was,

of course, as fast as the Mercedes would go.

The windshield wipers fought the rain with a hypnotic intensity. They made her drowsy, and her constant surveillance of the car behind her didn't help.

She thought of stopping at Perleburg, the three-quarter mark, but vetoed it and drove on. At Ludwigslust, she spotted the sign for Highway 106 and headed north toward Schwerin. The road narrowed here, and, because it was tightly hemmed with trees, it was also much darker.

She was forced to slow her speed to fifty miles per hour.

The Volvo had dropped far back, but its lights were still visible in the distance.

Suddenly, from a rest area turn-out, a large Mercedes sedan swerved onto the road and took the lane directly beside her. There were two men in the car, and out of the corner of her eye, Ursula could see them glancing over at her.

She speeded up, and so did they. She slowed, and so did they.

Ahead about two miles, the road narrowed to enter a tunnel. Its thick concrete sides gleamed in the glare of the oncoming lights.

Behind her, she could see the lights—she assumed they belonged to the Volvo—picking up speed and coming on fast.

Ursula increased her speed. Suddenly there was no room. The sedan was edging toward her.

She lifted her foot from the accelerator and stomped on the brake pedal.

It was too late.

She had been traveling at eighty-five miles an hour. The brake had only slowed her to sixty when the nose of the little convertible smashed into the concrete side of the tunnel.

Carter watched Erhanee's fingers fly over the keyboard, and the letters and characters blip up and then disappear on the computer screen.

The Indian hadn't said so, but Carter could tell from the glazed look in the man's eyes that he was making progress.

"You've got it."

"Not quite, but I think I'm close. The access codes were simple. I just made them too hard. Get that, will you?"

Carter grabbed the phone. "*Ja?*"

"Herr Carter?"

By now Carter knew the raspy voice well. "Speaking. Have you got her?"

"I'm afraid not. My people were ready to move, but she left her flat and drove through the wall."

"To East Berlin?"

"No. She took the Number Fifteen autobahn to West Germany."

Carter was sweating. "That should have made the grab easier."

"It would have," Voigt answered, "if she had not crashed into the side of a tunnel."

"An *accident*?"

"It will appear so to the authorities. Two of my men were following her. They saw a large Mercedes sedan force the crash."

"She's dead," Carter hissed.

"Very. Her head went through the windshield, and her chest was crushed by the steering wheel."

"Your people didn't get the license number, did they?"

"Yes, but later."

"Later . . .?"

"Needless to say, they didn't remain at the scene. As they were returning, the Mercedes passed them on the East German autobahn. They saw it pull off an Nauen."

"In East Germany?" Carter gasped.

"Quite."

Voigt didn't need to elaborate. If the people who killed Ursula Rhinemann left the autobahn in East Germany, particularly at night, they were official.

"I assume, Herr Carter, that our agreement is now finished?"

"Ended, Herr Voigt. *Danke*."

"*Bitte*."

The connection was broken, and Carter eased the phone back to its cradle.

*Too many people dead, the connection with the East too strong.*

He was pretty sure he had it now. The killing of Ursula Rhinemann capped it. She was the last link that could put Stephan Conway in the hot seat.

"I've got it!"

Carter moved to stand behind Erhanee at the console. He already knew what had come up. The KGB had been ahead of him. They had figured the wrong-way kill, and laid it to Conway.

It was ten-to-one the future senator had played ball to save his own skin.

Erhanee confirmed it.

"There it is, the shipment, almost down to the last microchip you got from the Pentagon."

"Whose authorization code?"

"Personal, Stephan Conway."

"Where's it going?"

"Lufthansa out of Dulles. Lands at Frankfurt, five A.M. local time."

"They'll make the switch at the airport right after customs."

"It's scheduled to be shifted to a military transport to West Berlin."

"They'll have phony crates ready," Carter growled.

"That's your department, not mine," Erhanee said, turning to face Carter.

The Killmaster was already headed out the door.

The radio crackled in the aide's hand. He lifted it to his ear and spoke. When it was still, he turned to his superior.

"Comrade Colonel?"

"*Da.*"

"He is in the forbidden zone now, heading for the Mitte Gate."

"*Da*, I can see him," Balenkov replied, moving the high-powered glasses along with the hurrying man. "He is following instructions to the letter."

Bile boiled in Balenkov's belly. He himself had given

Dieter Klauswitz the instructions that would send him to his death.

"I am afraid, Herr Klauswitz, that we cannot afford to allow you to leave East Berlin aboard Aeroflot. However, you are free to reenter West Berlin. The Mitte Gate will be kept open for your crossing. Once back in the West, I am sure your American papers will still be enough to allow your escape."

Balenkov moved the binoculars to the closed gate and then back to Klauswitz. The man had spotted the deserted gate. The colonel, from his rooftop observation post, could almost see the fear and realization on the killer's face.

Klauswitz whirled, his eyes searching the raked sand of no-man's-land between the two walls. His mind now knew that he had been deceived. But he was still loose. How could he get over the wall and grab a second chance at freedom?

He couldn't.

His only choice was the East German countryside.

He walked away from the wall and began to run.

Then it happened.

A blinding white glare blasted the street and the running figure. Staccato bursts of gunfire broke the night stillness.

Klauswitz fell, rolled, and came to his feet again. He staggered.

There was another short burst, and he fell.

This time he didn't move.

"The casket is ready?"

"*Da*, Comrade Colonel."

"I will inform the SSD that the assassin has been killed while trying to escape. Also, that we have a signed confession that he attempted to kill Stephan Conway."

"Comrade Colonel Palmitkov is a thorough woman," the aide said, pride in his voice.

"Yes, isn't she," Balenkov replied drily, and added mentally, *Aren't we all very efficient killing machines?*

Carter smoked and peered through the little waves of rain that trickled down the windshield. Beside him, Bruchner fidgeted in the seat. Marty Jacobs sat quietly in the back.

They were in one of the oldest and grubbiest sections of Frankfurt, staring at an old, grubby warehouse.

Knowing what to look for had made spotting the switch at the warehouse easy. Cartons of everyday radio gear had been switched with the Protec equipment. The four Protec crates had been relabeled and loaded on a truck with the rest of the nonclassified gear.

Four of Bruchner's men were already waiting to pounce on the cargo handlers who had made the switch.

The three of them had followed the truck to this warehouse. Now they waited.

"Someone's coming . . . it's a van!"

"I see it," Carter said, mashing out his cigarette.

The van pulled up to the wide double doors, and someone stepped from the driver's side. There was movement in front of the van's headlights, and the doors swung open. The figure turned, and for a brief moment was fully illuminated.

"Jesus Christ," Marty Jacobs hissed. "It's Anna Palmitkov herself!"

"It sure as hell is," Carter growled as the van entered the building and the doors closed behind it. "Now a lot of things are clear."

*And all bets are off*! he thought, sliding from the car.

"Both of you stay here. This one's private!"

Neither man moved.

Carter crossed the wet pavement to the side door of the warehouse away from the main double doors.

He had already jimmied the lock, so he was able to slip in quietly and quickly. He removed his shoes and made his way through piles of boxes stacked on wooden pallets.

She was just pulling the last crate off the truck. She moved quickly, efficiently. The cardboard crates were bulky but not heavy. She picked one up easily and headed for the van.

Carter slipped in behind her and waited until she dropped back to the floor.

"I told you to stay in Russia, comrade."

Her face registered shock and surprise. With obvious effort she got control of herself and spoke in a small tight voice. "It will make no difference. We have the proof on Conway.

If this shipment doesn't go through, he will find a way to get another to us rather than ruin his future."

"I've already figured that, Anna," Carter said, moving toward her as he jacked a shell into Wilhelmina's chamber but left the safety on. "That's why I'll make a deal. I want Conway."

"Oh?"

"That's right. What have you got on him?" She told him, and Carter nodded. "I figured that. We trade. You give me the means to squash Conway, and you can have the Protec boxes."

"Do you think I'm a fool, Carter? Besides, the photographs and confessions are in East Berlin. I don't have them to trade."

"Then I'll just kill you and do whatever I can to get Conway."

She shrugged and stepped to the right, away from the van's open doors. Carter lifted the gun. He wasn't going to fire, he was going to bluff.

He wanted to kill her, but alive she might still be the key to getting Conway.

She read him like a book.

With a rapid movement, she darted around the side of the van and headed for the big double doors.

Jolted by her sudden action, Carter didn't catch her until she was almost at the door. He grabbed her waist with one arm just as their momentum slammed them both into the closed doors.

She was good, and fast—maybe even faster than Carter.

She recovered first, twisted, and jabbed a knee toward his groin. He blocked it with his thigh. She grabbed for the hand that held Wilhelmina, fingers clawing with surprising strength. Her finger jammed his through the trigger guard. But the safety was still on.

Changing tactics, she roatated her hips into his stomach and prepared to throw him. Carter knew from past experience that she was as strong as a man, and fought with quiet desperation.

He blocked the attempted throw and twisted the gun out of

her grasp. It was a mistake. She heeled his instep, snapped the back of her head into his face, and clawed at his groin with both hands.

His eyes teared and he felt blood rushing from his mashed nose. A silent scream rose in his choking throat as her squeezing fingers found his testicles.

Involuntarily his hand opened, dropping Wilhelmina to the concrete. Her gasps of exertion turned to grunts as she squeezed harder and dropped to one knee. Like a snake, one hand freed him and darted to the Luger. In the same movement, he saw her flip the safety to "off" and bring the gun upward.

She meant to level the barrel over her own shoulder, and he could see that it was about to work.

He had no choice.

His right arm encircled her throat, and her straining gasps were stilled. The gun was at her shoulder now, and his arm tightened over her throat. Slowly the hand at his groin relaxed, but she still tried to take blind aim with the Luger.

He applied more pressure, and at last she went limp.

He squeezed one last time to make sure, and then let her lifeless body settle to the concrete floor. He tugged a handkerchief from his pocket and wiped the tears from his eyes and the blood from his face as he looked down at the still form.

She hadn't moved. His fingers found the carotid artery in her neck. There was no pulse. She was dead.

"I warned you, Anna," he said, and staggered to the doors.

The moment he was outside, he could see Bruchner and Marty Jacobs running toward him.

"Did you . . .?" Jacobs said.

"She's dead," Carter croaked. "The Protec boxes are on the truck. Load them and her in our car."

He headed for a phone booth on the corner. Behind him, he could hear Bruchner's voice. "Did you get anything out of her we can use on Conway?"

"No," Carter growled over his shoulder. "The son of a bitch is away clean."

It took him five minutes to get through to West Berlin and Horst Vintner. In terse sentences he laid out the last two hours to the SSD man.

"So the only way we can get the bastard is to get our hands on Klauswitz. Call over the wall, and don't tell them sweet Anna's dead. *Do* tell them we've got her, and we'll trade."

There was a long pause on the other end of the line, and then what amounted to a low groan. "Klauswitz is on his way over now," Vintner said. "In a box."

"Shit," Carter groaned.

"But don't worry about Conway," Vintner said, his voice almost a whisper. "Lisa Berrington emptied a 9mm Beretta into him in his hotel room a half hour ago."

Carter froze, his mind whirling. He should have known . . . Hong Kong . . . her mood . . . He should have known.

"Were there any witnesses?"

"I thought the same thing," Vintner replied. "But there's nothing we can do. She shot him in front of five people."

Carter didn't even reply. He just dropped the phone back on its cradle and started back toward the warehouse. Suddenly he stopped, lit a cigarette, and changed his mind.

He turned on his heel and began walking into the rain. It was almost dawn, and the light didn't make the streets any less grubbier.

# DON'T MISS THE NEXT NEW
# NICK CARTER SPY THRILLER


## *MERCENARY MOUNTAIN*


One tall man, his tattered rags flapping over his black skin, his turban so filthy it was impossible to believe it had ever been white, his skin so dusty it was more gray than black, staggered after the vanished patrol, drawn like a moth to the sound of their passage, pulled inexorably by their very speed, their power. An animal following anything that moved in the hope of food.

The rear soldier of the patrol glanced back at the road and the river of refugees and saw the ragged peasant weaving and struggling after them, his eyes rolled up to the sky as if blind, his mouth open and gasping for air. The soldier dropped back and kicked the refugee's feet out from under him. The ragged man crashed down into the dust and brush and lay motionless.

"Eat dirt, pig," the soldier muttered. "It will teach you not to defy your leaders."

The soldier hurried back to his post at the rear of the patrol. The column vanished on through the brush. Silence descended on the mountainside. There was only the shuffle of feet down on the barren road, and the cries of birds in the dry trees.

The peasant raised his head. The eyes that had been turned blindly up to the sky quickly surveyed the hidden hillside. He was alone. He leaped to his feet, moved off the trail, and ran forward in a silent, ground-covering stride parallel to the path. He seemed to glide like a snake through the thick brush, as silent as a ghost, and as unseen.

He caught up with the hurrying patrol down on the path and then settled into an effortless, long-striding walk parallel to the soldiers. Together they moved on up the mountainside, the soldiers single-file on the narrow trail, the ragged, unseen peasant twenty yards up the side of the mountain among the thick brush and trees.

A mile in from the road the officer raised his hand in a small clearing on the mountainside. The patrol came to a sharp halt. The officer looked, listened, and then signaled his men to take up positions around the perimeter of the small clearing. The officer sat down with his back against a thick tree, lit a long Russian cigarette, and blew lazy streams of smoke. He seemed to be waiting, was in no hurry, enjoying his ease and his cigarette.

Up on the side of the mountain the still unseen peasant in the ragged turban watched.

The sharp call of a bird came from somewhere ahead along the trail.

The officer in the clearing sat up, his cigarette held motionless.

On the mountain the hidden peasant listened.

The call of the bird came again. It was a good imitation, but to the ears of the peasant, not quite good enough. The officer in the clearing waited for a third call. Then he cupped his hands and gave a return call.

The officer stood, motioning order to his men. They spread out through the trees to cover the clearing. The officer watched the trail ahead. His slender black hand rested on the butt of his pistol.

Two men came into the clearing.

On the mountainside the peasant aimed a powerful pair of binoculars at the pair. They came into focus as they were greeted by the patrol officer. He could see that one was an Ethiopian general, and the second a short, stocky civilian wearing a khaki bush jacket with the symbol of a U.N. observer on its breast pocket.

He moved the binoculars to observe the civilian's right hand with its four rings. The stocky man's left hand was missing the tip of the third finger. Then he studied the tall, erect general with his smart khaki uniform and Sam Browne belt despite the heat and the rugged country. He returned the binoculars to their pocket in his filthy turban and withdrew a small, rectangular case from under his ragged robes.

As the general, the civilian, and the patrol officer conferred in the center of the clearing under the guns of the alert soldiers of the patrol, the hidden watcher on the mountainside opened the case and assembled a short, compact rifle with a telescopic sight. Prone, he aimed at the conference in the clearing below.

"Ahhhhhnnnnnnnnnhhnnnnnnnnnnnnnnn!"

The scream of agony shattered the forest. A cloud of birds rose into the air from the dry trees. Animals scurried through the thick brush. In the clearing the soldiers stared along the trail from where the general and the civilian had come.

"Nnnnnnhhhhhhh . . ."

The groan of pain strangled into silence at the edge of the clearing where two soldiers appeared dragging something torn and red and bleeding. Its face was a mass of purplish-black bruises and blood, its clothing so ripped and bloody it was almost unrecognizable as clothing, the thing itself almost unrecognizable as a man. But it was a man, beaten and tortured into something no longer human.

The general's voice carried across the distance.

"Well?"

One of the soldiers dragging the nearly unconscious man answered.

"He would say nothing more, General."

"Oh? Then why do we need him?"

The tall general, immaculate in his starched uniform and Sam Browne belt, drew his pistol, posed for a moment with the barrel against the unconscious man's bloody head, and fired. The two soldiers let the body fall into the forest dirt.

On the mountainside the hidden man fired his compact rifle in the echo of the execution.

In the clearing the civilian in the bush jacket with the U.N. emblem was hurled backward and fell heavily, his arms flung out, his eyes staring up at the thick mass of branches of the forest roof, blood soaking into the dirt around his head.

"Up there!" the patrol officer shouted.

The soldiers rushed toward the rise of the mountain. The ragged man picked off two before they had taken three steps, bloody brain matter and bone fragments splattering over those behind them. The others dived for cover. The general fell behind a tree.

"Get me out of here!" he bawled.

The patrol officer turned. "But, General, up there—"

"The hell with whoever's up there! Get your men around me and get me away from here now!"

The younger officer barked commands. The soldiers half scurried, half crawled backward away from the slope of the mountain to where the general waited behind his tree. The young Ethiopian officer looked back to where the hidden peasant watched. Disgust written all over him, he motioned to his men. With the general cowering in the middle of them, they marched back down the trail toward the distant road and the endless stream of refugees.

There was silence in the forest.

Even the birds were gone.

The tall man on the slope stood up in his filthy turban and tattered native clothing. He listened for some time. There was no sound. Nothing moved. Down in the dusty clearing the four bodies lay with their blood still spreading around them. Slowly the birds began to call, sing, cry to each other high in the trees. Animals moved warily in the brush. The man with the sniper rifle walked down the mountainside to the clearing.

He stood for a time looking off in the direction where the patrol and the general had vanished. He laughed out loud.

"That's one general who values his own skin," he said to the trees and brush and now singing birds.

Then he bent to examine the two dead civilians. He studied first the one in the bush jacket whom he had shot himself. He stripped the body, searching the clothes swiftly but thoroughly with all the skill of a man trained and experienced in locating hidden objects. He turned to the naked body itself and finally extracted a slender steel needle from under the skin over the dead man's shoulder blade. He slipped the needle into a hidden slot in his ragged sandals, then turned to the beaten and tortured man executed with the single shot to the head.

Even his cool eyes seemed to wince as he saw the extent of the dead civilian's injuries. But they were the eyes of a man who had seen much of what man can inflict on his fellowman, and he went back to his work of searching this body. He came up with a thin wallet and took a card from the wallet. He stared at the blood-smeared card for some time. Then his quick eyes looked past the card and the dead man to the ground under the corpse's right hand. There in the hard dust and dirt, the executed man had traced a single word in his own blood:

MAMBA

—From MERCENARY MOUNTAIN
A New Nick Carter Spy Thriller
From Charter in March 1986

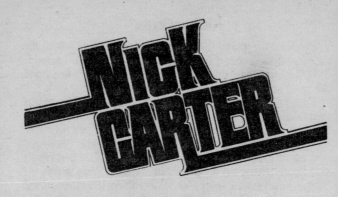

| | | |
|---|---|---|
| ☐ 03211-7 | **THE ASSASSIN CONVENTION** | $2.50 |
| ☐ 05386-6 | **THE BERLIN TARGET** | $2.50 |
| ☐ 06790-5 | **BLOOD OF THE SCIMITAR** | $2.50 |
| ☐ 06861-8 | **THE BLUE ICE AFFAIR** | $2.50 |
| ☐ 14222-2 | **DEATH HAND PLAY** | $2.50 |
| ☐ 21877-6 | **THE EXECUTION EXCHANGE** | $2.50 |
| ☐ 57280-4 | **THE KILLING GROUND** | $2.50 |
| ☐ 45520-4 | **THE KREMLIN KILL** | $2.50 |
| ☐ 24089-5 | **LAST FLIGHT TO MOSCOW** | $2.50 |
| ☐ 51353-0 | **THE MACAO MASSACRE** | $2.50 |
| ☐ 52276-9 | **THE MAYAN CONNECTION** | $2.50 |
| ☐ 57502-1 | **NIGHT OF THE WARHEADS** | $2.50 |
| ☐ 58612-0 | **THE NORMANDY CODE** | $2.50 |
| ☐ 69180-3 | **PURSUIT OF THE EAGLE** | $2.50 |
| ☐ 74965-8 | **SAN JUAN INFERNO** | $2.50 |
| ☐ 79822-5 | **TARGET RED STAR** | $2.50 |
| ☐ 79831-4 | **THE TARLOV CIPHER** | $2.50 |
| ☐ 88568-3 | **WHITE DEATH** | $2.50 |

Prices may be slightly higher in Canada.